The Sandling Case
What Would You Have Done?

By Louis Tracy

Originally published in 1928

The Sandling Case
What Would You Have Done?

Published by Resurrected Press

This classic book was handcrafted by Resurrected Press. Resurrected Press is dedicated to bringing high quality classic books back to the readers who enjoy them. These are not scanned versions of the originals, but, rather, quality checked and edited books meant to be enjoyed!

Please visit ResurrectedPress.com to view our entire catalogue!

ISBN 13: 978-1-937022-20-4

Printed in the United States of America

OTHER RESURRECTED PRESS MYSTERIES

FOREWORD

Louis Tracy's *The Sandling Case* blends two genres, the mystery and the tale of intrigue. Espionage was a popular theme for novelists in the years immediately before, during and after World War I and many mystery writers tried their hand at it, including Agatha Christie in her second novel, *The Secret Adversary*. Spies, secret formulas, and plans for powerful new weapons became as much the fodder for novels as jewel thefts and murder. It is no surprise then, that Tracy, who wrote a great deal of historical romances and adventure novels should be tempted to base a novel around such an idea.

Of all the new weapons that appeared during World War I, the airplane, the tank, the submarine, none was as feared as poison gas. Far too many of the soldiers fighting in the trenches suffered permanent debilitating injuries from this insidious weapon for it not to take horrific root in the popular mind. Only the advent of the atomic bomb in the following war was able to displace it from the public psyche. The idea of a gas that could turn an entire battlefield into an incendiary inferno would certainly have been something the average reader would perceive as a dire threat. That the gas in the novel, methane, was neither secret nor a particularly weaponizable threat, just shows that Tracy was a better writer than chemist.

Captain Mannering finds himself taken under the tutelage of that pair of famous detectives, Chief Superintendent Winter and Detective Inspector Furneaux of Scotland Yard. This pair first appeared as minor characters in *The Stowmarket Mystery*, but later became one of Tracy's most favorite vehicles appearing in number of his mysteries including *The Strange Case of Mortimer Fenley* and *The Postmaster's Daughter*. Unlike most detectives who operated alone or with a sidekick or chronicler like Holmes and Watson, Winter and Furneaux always act as a team of equals, though Winter is technically the superior officer and Furneaux the greater intellect. Mostly, the two spend their time hurling jibes and insults at each other, particularly when they are hot on the heels of some criminal. So fond was Tracy of this entertaining pair that he used a thinly veiled version of them in *The Bartlett Mystery* a novel set in New York, and in *The House of Peril* he actually transformed them into New York detectives. In a curious twist, Tracy rewrote the latter for the British edition as The Park Lane Murder restoring the pair to their proper London locale.

Detectives weren't all that Tracy liked to recycle. The Italian restaurant, "Pucci's," which appears in The House of Peril reappears in *The Sandling Case* transported to Soho, London complete with owner and passwords, as Winter and Furneaux's favorite hangout.

The Sandling Case is an entertaining and fast paced mystery, and Resurrected Press is happy to offer it for our readers' enjoyment. *The Sandling Case* has also appeared as *What Would You Have Done?*.

About the Author

Louis Tracy (1863-1928) was a British journalist and author. He wrote numerous books both under his own name and using the pseudonyms Gordon Holmes and Robert Fraser. He shared these pseudonyms and collaborated with P.M. Shiel on a number of works. Among his books are *The Wings of Morning* (1903), *The Stowmarket Mystery* (1904), and *Number Seventeen* (1916).

Greg Fowlkes
Editor-In-Chief
Resurrected Press
www.ResurrectedPress.com

TABLE OF CONTENTS

CHAPTER 1: WHY THE GIRL IN THE CAR TURNED BACK

A SUSPICIOUS country policeman, reporting to his district superintendent certain tragic happenings which he was wholly unable to account for, described Robert Mannering as "a man of good appearance who spoke like a gentleman." That was later in the day, however—say, an hour or more after Mannering raised his eyes from close scrutiny of a small-scale map to gaze in surprise at a heavy bank of black cloud travelling swiftly over the moor from the south-west.

"Wow, wow, and likewise wuff!" said the map-reader aloud, springing upright from a wayside rock. "If that isn't a front-rank thunder storm, I've never seen one; so it's me for the beaten track and some sort of burrow— even a cow-byre."

Without a second's delay he struck into the long, swift strides demanded by a pace of five miles an hour. The straight road in front led through an undulating stretch of moorland. On the right, the heather clothed the flanks of one of the highest hills in Yorkshire. On the left, but at a much greater distance, the crest of another giant seemed to bound the plateau crossed by the road. But appearances are deceptive in great open spaces. The map had been clear enough on this point. Somewhere on that side, probably a mile beyond an upward curve in the heather, a deep valley held a tiny hamlet famous for an ancient church and a Norman crypt.

Mannering, versed in the tricks of a wild country, reasoned that the ground fell too steeply to permit even a bridle-path to cut straight across the moor. But there might. be some narrow cleft down which a sure-footed pedestrian could scramble. Herein the map's contour lines were vague. He had sat down to study them carefully when a sudden darkness warned him of the change in the weather.

He knew there was a village three miles ahead. If he got soaked to the skin, it was only common sense that he should elect for human habitation and a reasonable prospect of drying his clothes rather than be caught in a waste of heather, where the driving rain would obliterate all landmarks, and one ran grave risk of falling into a peat-hole.

On the right front the ground sloped slightly downward from the road—sure sign that at the foot of the hill was a bog. That did not interest him at all; he must stick to the road. He soon found some crude evidences of an enclosed pasture. Beyond lay a dense plantation of black firs.

Tucked into a hollow beneath the wood, the brick chimneys and red-tiled roof of a moorland farm showed up unexpectedly. The building was so hidden as to be hardly visible from any other point than a very small section of the highway.

"By Jove!" cried Mannering. "What luck!"

He took to his heels and literally raced the oncoming storm. Even so, he noticed two things—a pack of grouse scurrying low over the neighbouring hill, and an astonishingly new white painted gate at the junction of road and wood. He saved a good fifty yards, however, by jumping a tumbled-down dry wall and taking a diagonal course towards a rickety gate, which opened into an enclosure around the house. The short cut saved him a thorough drenching. He sprinted along a moss-grown path, bounded by neglected shrubs and overgrown herbaceous plants elbowed by rank weeds, and literally leaped into a squat outer porch as the first huge raindrops fell.

A dazzling flash of lightning heralded an ominously low and near crash of thunder. Then the rain came in a deluge; no mere shower, but a veritable cloudburst. The noise of its pelting on trees, earth, and house was deafening. In a few seconds a turbulent yellow stream was foaming past the porch and lipping the raised step which had been cunningly placed there many a year ago for the very purpose of defeating such unpleasant intrusions.

More lightning, even louder thunder, and a seemingly denser downpour caused a terrifying din. Mannering was inured to the fierce storms of North-East Assam—that breeding-place of elemental strife—but he had never seen or heard anything much worse than this almost phenomenal display in Yorkshire.

Turning his back on the outer racket, he knocked at a stout door, saying to himself with a quiet laugh: "Thank goodness I'm in the twentieth century. The good folk who lived here when this old house was built would surely have imagined that the devil himself had arrived!"

He knocked sharply enough with his knuckles, and then rapped with a stout oak stick, but there came no sign of life from the interior. At last he pressed the sneck of the latch. The door was locked; nay, more, barred so securely that it might as well have been a mere dummy in the surrounding masonry.

"No one at home—not even the dog," commented Mannering, facing the storm once more.

The porch was fairly roomy, some six feet by four. Small windows at each side revealed walls a foot thick. Outer entrance and doorway alike were pointed arches. Stout wooden seats had been fitted on either hand. Facing eastward, it would be a pleasant nook on a fine morning if the perennial plants and shrubs bordering the stone path were kept in order.

While darting towards his refuge, Mannering had noted that paved tracks flanked the house to right and left. The first entered a dilapidated farmyard, and probably led to the kitchen. The second ended at a wicket gate in a dense yew hedge, which prolonged the line of the building, so one might assume that a scrap of garden fronted the main rooms with their south aspect. The wood supplied an excellent screen from the east wind, and, assuming the existence of other hedges and trees, anyone occupying that side of the house would be completely shut off from sight or sound of the external world. Not even from the crest of the moor might the lower windows be seen.

Making the best of the enforced halt, Mannering loosened a buckle and allowed a well-filled rucksack to drop on one of the benches. He sat on the other, filled and lighted his pipe, and tried to estimate the progress and possible duration of the storm. The thunder, at any rate, was rolling away to the north, and the rain had ceased to be of tropical violence. The stream rushing past the porch puzzled him until he discovered that a small channel had actually been provided for it. Probably the lie of the land between house and bog determined the course of this necessary outlet for storm water and melting snow.

The place was inhabited—of that he was certain. Three deep-set windows, one on the ground floor and two in the upper story, were curtained. The wicket, like the larger gate by the road, had been painted recently. It was odd that the small gate at the actual entrance should be so out of repair. Still, it served its purpose, and he realised that the others were recent structures; hence their spick-and-span appearance. The paving, too, had been renewed in parts, and scratches on the original moss-covered stones told of the passing of hob-nailed boots.

It was a pity that the occupants had not devoted a little time and effort to clearing away weeds and trimming the borders. A few hours' work would have made the approach quite attractive.

He looked at his watch—three o'clock. Two hours ago he had left a wayside inn in the valley of the Esk and begun the steady climb which ended not far short of this lonely farm. He estimated he had walked nearly five miles. During the second part of the tramp he had not passed a house of any kind, and the nearest village was still three miles away. What an isolated spot this was! Anyone who lived here permanently must be content to lead the life of an anchorite. It was more than likely that the farm, as such, had long since ceased to exist, while the present tenant, or tenants, might use it as a summer residence, for which purpose it was admirably situated, if sheer privacy and the wild beauty of the high moors were alone desired.

The rain diminished to a drizzle, and the sky line to eastward became dimly visible. Five minutes later the greys and blacks of the August landscape changed magically to a gorgeous blend of vivid emerald and purple, with patches of scarlet and yellow among the brown of the heather. This glowing panorama might never have experienced such unpleasant things as thunderclouds and scourging rain. Even the diminishing rivulet began to gurgle cheerfully, the twitter of birds came from among the firs, and a nearby cock crowed a merry greeting to the sun. So Mannering' s guess had been correct. If utility fowls are to live in England there must be human beings to tend them.

"Well, I'm much obliged for your hospitality," said he, rising and nodding to the stubborn door.

He shouldered his pack, refilled his pipe, and was halfway along the garden path when some itch of curiosity impelled him to peep, as it were, at the hitherto invisible sides of the building. Turning back, he found, as he expected, that the farmyard was in a state of almost complete desuetude, save for a wire-netted run behind the empty stables. A number of White Leghorns were strut ting forth already from a smart and up-to-date fowl- house.

A strip of cleared land sloped down to the bog, whose existence he had assumed, and he saw now that the house and its immediate surroundings stood on a definite ridge, which skirted the west side of the plantation, so the casual torrent had followed the only available course, and was emptying itself into the bog a couple of hundred yards away.

A kitchen door was closed, but a long, low, uncurtained window invited a passing look. A deal table, some chairs, a dresser with crockery on the upper shelves and some cooking utensils in open divisions beneath, a pile of logs, and a sort of bin filled with coal bespoke occupancy. Indeed, Mannering was minded to make straight-way for the high-road when the mere whim of the moment led his feet past the porch to the wicket in the hedge. Here was a genuine surprise. Leaning over the gate he found himself gazing at a well-kept lawn and pretty garden. Two circular flower-beds glowed with geraniums, calceolarias, and lobelia. Hollyhocks, sunflowers, lupins, and marguerite daisies were banked against clusters of laurels and rhododendrons, while more delicate shrubs and plants were interspersed with the hardier growths. A right-angled strip of stout firs and a privet hedge shut off this gay oasis from every wind that blew, thus rendering possible the seemingly impossible— a bright pleasance in the midst of a bleak moor nearly a thousand, feet above the level of the not far distant sea.

And there were other astonishing features. A pair of double French windows had been thrust boldly through the old stone wall of the house, They, too, were ultra-modern in style and paint. A neat lattice-work of gnarled wood surrounded them and bore a wealth of climbing roses and wistaria. Even the sills of the small, unaltered windows of the rooms above held boxes of blue Dutch tiles filled with mignonette.

Somewhat guiltily now—for he felt that he was really trespassing—Mannering glanced around before passing through the wicket. The outer gate was visible clear of the wood, and there was no one in sight, so, yielding to temptation, he determined to steal a glimpse of the interior of this oddly contradictory dwelling. He had no unworthy motive. He merely fancied that he might learn something of the manners and ways of the house's owners by the aspect of what was evidently a spacious and well-lighted living-room.

But he met with a check. Heavy, dark-blue blinds were lowered behind each window. Again he was retreating when, by idle chance, he noticed a disturbing thing. Four panes of glass, together with their cross of wooden frame, had been forced outwards from the second window. Shattered wood and splintered glass were eloquent of a fierce struggle or a strange accident within the room, and no observant eye could fail to notice that the material of the blind was neither cut nor scratched, so it had been pulled down after the window was broken.

Mannering was not a nervous subject. Probably few men of his years—thirty-two, all told—had been trained in a more rigorous school, for he had gone straight from four years of war in Europe to eight years of hard endeavour in the hill jungles of Assam and Upper Burmah. But, suddenly and almost unaccountably, despite the peaceful surroundings of that sunlit garden, he sensed a tragedy lurking behind those drawn blinds.

He did not hesitate, of course. Instant decision, whether in great events or small, had become a habit to which he had owed his life many times. Removing a large section of glass ready to fall at touch, he sought for and found the handle of the upright iron rod fastening the two sections of the window, which he opened sufficiently to reach the bottom of the blind. A slight pull, and it shot upward, though he did not fail to grasp the check cord in case it overran the controlling spring.

Then he saw what he feared, yet half expected, to see—the dead body of a man stretched in front of a fireplace in the centre of the west wall!

On that side of the house, in the extreme angle of the room, a tall, narrow window gave added light. It had a blind, like the others, but an open fanlight, a mere slit, as it were, useless for a burglar's purposes, compelled the roller to be adjusted beneath its hinges, and, at that hour, the sun's rays were already streaming in. So Mannering had no difficulty whatever in determining that the man, an elderly man, dressed in a rough homespun as expensive as any broad cloth, and wearing well-cut shoes and brown silk stockings, had been battered to death most brutally.

He was sprawled awkwardly, face downwards, with his feet near to where Mannering stood. Blows seemed to have been rained on him, and a heavy poker had evidently broken the back of his skull, because grey hairs were still adhering to it where it had been thrown into the hearth. His clothes were torn, too, so he must have fought hard. Chairs were overturned and smashed. A china vase and clock had been swept off the mantelpiece; Mannering saw that the hands of the clock had stopped at half-past two.

Again this passer-by proved himself no weakling. Without ever a thought to the possible consequences if he were discovered in what was certainly a compromising situation, he stepped into the room, lifted the dead man's head, ascertained by a glance at the eyes that death was really there, and by flexing an arm decided that rigor mortis had not yet set in.

The clock was a mute but almost infallible witness. This ghastly crime had been committed barely fifteen minutes before the storm had driven him, a complete stranger, into the shelter of the porch. So the person, or persons, responsible for this crime could not have gone far when he sprinted along the road. Most certainly they had not passed him, nor had anyone followed that straight and level track in the other direction during many minutes earlier, or he must have seen them. He could not help thinking of the murderers in the plural. The dead man was powerfully built. He had not been taken wholly unaware. He had defended himself. Probably he was grappling with one assailant when another had struck a coward's blow with the poker, though, indeed, the mere use of such an implement argued a quarrel, lack of premeditation, frenzy, rather than criminal intent.

Then Mannering remembered that some grouse had been disturbed on the crest of the hill beyond the bog. That was it. The criminals had made off through the heather to the north west. Even so, had he not been so absorbed in that stupid map, he could hardly have failed to notice them, though, to be sure, his mind was occupied by the topographical problem set by the other side of the road.

He would have liked to examine the house most thoroughly, but none knew better than he that every second was precious now. He must hurry to the village and raise a hue and cry.

And that is exactly what he did do—twenty minutes later! During that interval he passed through many unnerving experiences. He had seen death staring him in the face, not once, but several times.

At any rate, he escaped, and was completely successful in getting away from the accursed place unobserved—he was sure of that. Once on the road, he ran a good quarter of a mile before looking back. He found he could not see the gate owing to the low-lying branches of the trees, but no one was either watching or following him. There was a slight dip in the road a little ahead, so, before entering it, he took another look. All was well. He estimated that he could come in sight again about a hundred yards farther on, but by that time he would be nearly half a mile from the entrance to the farm. He had, in fact, reached that point, and had again made fairly certain that he was not pursued, when the steady beat of an engine driven at normal speed told that a car was approaching.

He slowed from a jog-trot to a walk. Being rather breathless and excited, he wanted to be collected enough to appeal for help without alarming the people in the car.

He took it for granted that no one would be driving alone along a road which in August attracted only the more sedate type of tourists, so he was dismayed, almost irritated, when he found that the oncoming motorist was a lady, whose sole companion was a fox-terrier. Still, he had to make the best of a queer business, and try to explain the urgency of his requirements without creating a suspicion that he was a sensa tion-monger, if not a veritable lunatic.

So he signalled in good time that he wanted a word, though he believed that the lady herself was of the same mind, because the engine slowed before he raised his hand.

The car was an open two-seater with a dicky, in which a couple of leather suitcases were housed. The dog barked in a friendly way, as though he were entitled to open the conversation.

"Oh, do keep quiet, Tags!" commanded his owner, an apparently self-possessed young woman who was by way of being remarkably good looking.

"Can you tell me," she went on, examining the man with a candid stare, "if there is a farm house in the hollow behind that plantation on the left?"

To Mannering's ears at that moment the whole wide range of the English language could not have yielded a more surprising question.

"Yes," he said. "Are you thinking of going there?"

"Yes. I'm a bit late, too. I must push on. Did you want anything?"

Thus far he had been standing a little on one side. He drew nearer, and rested a foot on the off-side running-board, stooping, too, seemingly to ease the weight of the ruck-sack.

"You must have passed through a village a little over two miles away. Did you happen to notice if a police-constable is stationed there?" he said.

The girl smiled at that.

"Yes," she answered, readily enough, for Mannering was one of those men in whom all women, children, and dogs place instant confidence. "He was at the door of his cottage, which was labelled. Indeed, he told me how to reach Blackdown Farm. I should have arrived there fully half an hour ago, but was held up by the thunderstorm."

"Are you, like me, a stranger in this locality?"

"I don't mind telling you that I have never been here before," but her tone stiffened, and her hand fell to the clutch.

"Please listen to what I have to say, and believe it," said Mannering gravely, turning to look back along the road as though he expected some evil thing to appear. "You cannot go to the farm. There has been a tragedy. I want you to take me, without another moment's delay, to that policeman. Then, if you choose, you can hear what I have to tell him."

"This is nonsense!" protested the girl, with heightened colour.

Sh was not alarmed in the least, which was satisfying. She merely resented being told she must act thus and so without any option on her part.

"No. It is most distressingly true," insisted Mannering.

"Are you a friend of Mr. Hope's?" she demanded.

"If that is the name of the elderly man now lying dead in the farm, I am not."

"Dead! Do you really mean that?"

"Yes. I cannot tell you how sorry I am to be forced to blurt out the facts in this open-mouthed way. Nor can I offer an explanation. I am beholden to you for the names of both the house and its occupant. But Mr. Hope, or someone residing there, was killed about an hour ago, and "—here Mannering's brows furrowed slightly, for he had never ceased to keep an eye on the edge of the wood—" unless I am greatly mistaken, one of the two men who, I am sure, are responsible for his death is now watching us from the gate which leads to the house. Possibly he heard your car, and wondered why it had stopped. Now, more strongly than ever, I demand that you take me to the village."

The girl was a little frightened, perhaps, but she was annoyed, too.

"If what you say is true, cannot we do something other than run away?" she asked, with just a hint of scorn in her voice. "There are two of us, and Tags will tackle an elephant if I bid him."

"I have no doubt. The elephant would probably hook it, being usually a timid beast. I admit I am running away, for the excellent reason that an oak stick would make a poor show against a pair of automatic pistols. But I assure you I am coming back. And we must not waste more time. If you refuse me as a passenger, I shall travel as the driver."

"What on earth?"

"Please don't argue. I won't let you. I simply have to save you, and Tags as well, from very real danger. You can see for yourself how interested that chap is in our movements. So, to put matters plainly, unless you give in at once I shall grab Tags by the scruff of the neck and chuck him out, at the same time pushing you away from the wheel, using all the force that may be necessary. Tags must follow as best he can."

The girl actually laughed. Were she not face to face with a tragedy, she would probably have twitted him as acting like a cave-man.

"I really believe you mean it," she said. "Very well. Come round to the other side and hop in. Never mind the whelp. He's accustomed to being squeezed when the dicky is full."

Mannering passed in front of the car. The engine was running, so the girl might have knocked him over had she chosen.

"Thanks," he said, opening the door and giving the dog a chummy pat.

She ignored the tribute completely.

"I imagine that the man watching us from the gate will now get the wind up rather badly; of course, operations have not gone just as I wished, but that cannot be helped," he went on.

The car was backed and turned quite skilfully. Once headed the other way Mannering kept his eyes front. There was no sense in deliberately apprising the distant watcher that he had been seen.

"I don't quite understand," said the girl, when the engine was purring evenly.

"Well, my first scheme was to send to the village for assistance, and try meanwhile to keep tab on a pair of scoundrels at the farm; but that is impracticable now."

"You said nothing of it to me."

"No. I found you a trifle difficult. Moreover, I doubt whether the police-constable would have believed you, because, at the best, you could only have told a cock-and-bull story."

"Supplied by you."

"A fair retort. You see, I did not count on meeting a woman, so I have suppressed a lot of most unpleasant details."

"Such as?"

"I'll renew my offer. You can hear what I tell the policeman."

"Has Mr. Hope been murdered, then?"

"Yes, I think so. Indeed, I can go so far as to say I am certain of it."

"How horrible! I don't know him, but he wrote charming letters. He engaged me for some secretarial work. But—was he alone? He stated that a man and his wife ran the establishment and would look after me well during the next two months."

"There could hardly have been any other members of the household there when this affair took place, unless they, too, are dead. I look forward to getting some definite information on that and other points in the village. By the way, my name is Robert Mannering. During the past eight years I have been a sort of tea-planter and general roustabout in North-East India. Four days ago, at

Northallerton, I began a walking tour through the North Riding. Half an hour ago the trip might have come to a sudden and violent end."

"Were you attacked?"

"Oh no. There would have been no attack. I would merely have passed out before I knew what struck me."

"Then what would have happened to me if I had not met you?"

"I don't know. I can only hope that you might have been sent off again on some plausible pretext. I don't suppose those two thugs would have killed you in mere lust of killing. But they would not have spared you for one second if they thought you even suspected what they had done."

"It sounds awful, and quite thrilling. As you have given me your name you ought to know mine—Betty Hardacre—Miss Betty Hardacre, of course—assistant lecturer and demonstrator in applied science at the West Yorkshire College of Technology. That is why I am here to-day."

"Because of both reasons?"

Miss Hardacre was puzzled for an instant. Then her blue eyes glinted ominously.

"I am only clearing the ground before we meet the policeman," she said with cold precision. "My story; at least, will bear analysis. Mr. Hope—the name is a thin disguise adopted by an eminent scientist to shut out intruders—is a friend of the principal of my college. He is in need of skilled help for a couple of months. I was recommended for the job. It eats up the whole of my holiday and a bit more, I expect, but the work is of national importance, so, for many more than two reasons, I trust you are making a great mistake in saying that— that Mr. Hope is dead."

CHAPTER 2: THE ONLY WITNESS

MANNERING was holding the dog's collar. The car was roomy enough, but not so wide that the girl should be unaware of a sudden muscular tension of his right forearm.

"Hope?" he said, and his voice became almost harsh with restraint. "An eminent scientist? . . . Good Lord! You are not telling me that the man I found lying dead in that house is Sir William Hope Sandling, of Oxford?"

Now it was Miss Betty's turn to yield to excitement. Up to this moment she had not been wholly convinced that matters were so bad as this distinguished-looking wayfarer wanted to make out. She was genuinely startled, but kept her wits about her.

"Do you happen to know Sir William?" she countered.

"I have not seen him for twelve years. Oh, this is too ghastly for words! I—I might have recognised him. Yet I failed. Don't ask why, Miss Hardacre."

With a real effort he conquered his agitation.

"I think I see our village down there in the valley," he continued. "Will you forgive me if I suggest that you should endeavour to dissociate yourself from the inquiry which will start in a few minutes?"

"How is that possible?" she said. "I believe I know what you have in mind. I'm sure you are being kind and thoughtful. But I cannot picture our policeman letting either of us off so easily. He had a wary eye for me quarter of an hour ago. Now that I come to think of it, he may have been instructed to give Sir—well, I may as well admit that 'Mr. Hope' is Sir William—to give him any assistance in his power. . . My aunt, I am right for once! Here he comes now on his bicycle."

They were still a good half-mile from the village when the constable drew alongside. He halted, having recognised the car. Disregarding Mannering, he said surprisingly: "You are Miss Hardacre, I suppose, miss?"

"Yes."

The lady was astonished, and showed it.

"Couldn't you find the farm?"

"I did not go so far. This gentleman will explain."

Mannering had been thinking hard during the past minute. The shock of a most grave and far-reaching discovery in the mere identity of the dead man had, in a sense, cleared his brain. It was vitally essential now that this country policeman, who looked rather intelligent, and might be all the more awkward to deal with because of his shrewdness, should do the right thing at once and not blunder into what may be described as the orthodox, or Police Manual, method.

So, to Miss Hardacre's further bewilderment, Mannering adopted forthwith the quietly authoritative air of an officer addressing a subordinate.

"That is my name," he said, leaning over the wheel and giving the policeman a visiting card. "I retain my army rank, though I have been in the Political Service of the Government of India during the past eight years. Fortunately, we three know who 'Mr. Hope' is. Or, do you know?"

The constable squirmed slightly. He, on his part, had recognised the "Centurion," the leader who says "'Go,' and he goeth, and 'Come,' and he cometh."

"Well," he began.

"Yes, that is quite right. You were warned, I assume, that this young lady would take up certain duties at Blackdown Farm to-day? Now, I ask you to accept as true every word I utter. Don't question me at this stage. Above all things, follow my advice until we reach the farm. There you can act exactly as you like, and I undertake to place myself unreservedly at your disposal from that moment."

The policeman said nothing, having nothing to say.

With remarkable brevity, considering the amazing facts he had to relate, Mannering told his story. It served its immediate purpose, but subsequent events demand clearness of detail, and this, of course, was a sheer impossibility in the conditions. The condensed version, given rapidly in the open road, was more than enough to spur the law into action. What actually happened is now set forth in proper sequence.

When Mannering rose from his knees by the side of the dead man he realised that everything was against him if he tried to trace the murderers. The storm must have obliterated all footprints or the recent track of a vehicle, though, to be sure, if the fugitives had actually alarmed the grouse while crossing the moor any means of conveyance could be left out of reckoning.

So the village—at any rate, the nearest farm—became his immediate objective. He hurried out, lowered the blind and closed the window, thus leaving the place exactly as he found it, and made for the exit. He had eyes now for all movement, near or far. Not a twig could have stirred when a bird took flight, not a blade of grass have been displaced by the furtive scamper of a rabbit, but he must have noted it. Therefore, as his field of vision widened beyond the porch and the out buildings, he was frozen into immobility by seeing two men standing by the edge of the bog in the hollow. Even while he looked they turned in his direction, but he dropped so quickly that he was sure they had not noticed him.

And now, once more, he revealed that trait of prompt action which habit and necessity had made a part of his nature. Crouching, he reached the porch, and then, swiftly and noiselessly, treading in the watercourse, passed the yew hedge, entered the wood, and wormed his way among firs and undergrowth until he reached a point whence, well screened himself, he could command both the house and the cleared land bordering the bog.

By this time the newcomers were nearly hidden by the buildings, yet, luckily for him, since the incident affected his subsequent actions materially, they halted for a moment, and one, the taller of the two, took an automatic pistol from a hip pocket and placed it in the right-hand pocket of his coat, where, of course, it was more instantly accessible.

"So that's that!" was Mannering's grim comment. "Now I know what's coming to me if I butt in. Well, well I In this case, to be forewarned is almost to be fire-armed."

He had no shred of doubt now that the pair knew exactly what they would find in that darkened room, because, a few seconds after they had vanished, he heard the click of the kitchen lock when a key was turned. He changed his plan instantly. Instead of making for the high-road he stood fast. Even if these fellows were the most callous of criminals, why had they gone away and come back? That was puzzling. He could not account for it. But how sure they were of their ground! How little they counted on being discovered! For that matter, how little they cared! He really must wait and see what happened.

He was not kept long in suspense. Evidently the smaller man had entered the house, but his companion came out through the farmyard and was walking quickly past the porch with the apparent intention of making for the distant main gate when he seemed to detect something of interest inside the porch. He went in, but was not out of sight for more than a few seconds. When he reappeared he had an air of intense watchfulness, his right hand remained in his coat pocket, and his eyes were everywhere—they seemed even to pierce the very depths of the wood. Soon the watcher found something of interest on the path to the right. He followed it, and peered over the wicket leading to lawn and garden, exactly as Mannering had done.

Then the unseen scout squirmed. He had used and thrown aside at least six matches while seated in the porch during the storm. He had taken no pains whatsoever to conceal any possible footprints while passing to the wicket or crossing a lawn so rain-sodden that in all likelihood the spongy turf bore marks of his progress. It was almost certain, too, that the carpet inside the room would still be wet and muddy where he had stood.

Nevertheless, he was not to blame for such lack of precaution. It was not he who had committed a crime.

Though his idle jest had been justified, and the devil had really visited the lonely farm that day, how could any poor mortal have suspected that the Evil One was in possession already?

"My hat!" Mannering then said to himself; "this affair grows more interesting every moment. The lad is a born tracker. Where would I be now if I hadn't walked up that watercourse? Shot at sight, and serve me jolly well right!"

The gentleman fondling the automatic entered the garden, but Mannering did not move. The air was strangely still after the storm, and he would surely be heard if he tried to force a way through the wood. Fortune had favoured him when he took chances he was not aware of. Now that he understood his perilous position he must rely on his own wits to extricate himself from it.

Depending on most trustworthy ears, he knew that a tap on a pane and some few words purposely muffled to indistinctness brought about the raising of a blind and the opening of one of the French windows. A piece of glass fell with a crash.

"Don't be so damned clumsy!" growled a voice. Evidently the speaker himself was so disturbed or his nerves were so frayed that he ignored the precautions he would have imposed on another.

There was some response, because the same voice continued: "Oh, shut up! Someone has been here while we were fooling around on the moor. . . Look at these. . . . I found them in the porch. It's up to us..."

The words trailed away into silence. The window was closed, and the blind fell again.

"It seems to me," reflected Mannering cheerfully, "that my health will benefit if I get a little nearer that gate. Give me fifty yards' start and neither of those two will ever be able to send a bullet home."

He showed real woodcraft now. A fox could hardly have crept through the thickly interlaced pines more secretly. He had to stand nearer the edge of the wood in order to keep an eye on the house, but he chose his position well. He could see through the fronds of a well-grown tree, yet his outline was thoroughly merged in a network of branches with a background of impenetrable gloom.

The first sign of life within the house came when an upstairs window was lowered a few inches and a face appeared dimly. Another window was opened elsewhere.

"Not a bad dodge," agreed Mannering. "It's wonderful how the terrain widens from an observation post even a few feet above the general level."

He glanced at his wrist-watch, and was sur prised to find that the time was only fifteen minutes past three. What a lot of excitement had been crowded into ten minutes! This, he supposed, might be regarded as the very essence of thrilling drama—action without the aid of a spoken word, because the little that had been said only repeated the story told already in silence.

In a little while, perhaps a couple of minutes, the watcher at the window withdrew. The cause was soon forthcoming. The taller man emerged hurriedly from the farmyard and made for the outer gate, but not without a close scrutiny of the long grass and weeds bordering the wood. Ho even halted twice to examine obvious rabbit runs. This gave Mannering to think. The scout knew his work. If he chose to follow the emptying channel of the storm-water there was nothing to prevent him from finding the point where the spy, whose nearness he suspected, had begun to take cover.

"Dash it all!" said the quarry; "if this blighter is going right round the wood I'd better he ready to skip. He's no amateur. I'll say that much for him, even when he's in the dock."

Was it worth while to crawl out and see what the fellow was doing? No. This might be an ingenious ruse to flush the game, and there was an obvious chance that any movement among the grasses could be detected from the house. However, that difficulty soon righted itself. The man had only gone as far as the gate, probably to look up and down the road. He returned at once, still thoroughly on the alert, with that right hand clutching the butt of the unseen automatic, and re-entered the house, again by way of the kitchen.

Mannering was at last undecided how to act for the best. The minutes were flying, and the only practical measures to get this pair arrested and the whole affair officially investigated could be begun in a village three miles away. Yet he was loath to hurry off with such an incomplete story. It was all-important that he should know which direction the two took when, as he assumed, they finally abandoned the scene of their ghastly crime. Perhaps he might meet someone on the road and summon assistance in that way while he himself followed the trail. But the one thing he could not endure was inaction. He resolved to wait another five minutes—until 3.25, in fact, and then gain the road. He was in good trim, and reckoned he could trot the three miles in less than half an hour, supposing, that is, he had to go the full distance. There would be guns in the village, and hardy moorland folk ready to use them. He himself, acting under the nominal leadership of a policeman, if one were available, would direct their energies. They would be familiar with every path across the moors for miles around, and he had already memorised many details in the clothing and appearance of the tall man. The second scoundrel was more nebulous, but a dark brown suit, brown shoes, and a grey cloth cap were helpful, while he walked with a lilting step, carrying the right shoulder higher than the left. Both men wore loose-fitting motoring gauntlets.

The smaller man had been little in evidence thus far. Most likely he was ransacking the house, or, it might be, keeping guard while his companion prowled about, but this problem was solved when the two came out, becoming visible in the field beyond the cattle-sheds. They were carrying some heavy weight slung to a couple of poles, and tied with a rope. Mannering had to think hard before he realised that they had wrapped the body in a carpet and were about to dispose of it.

They moved quickly, and set their burden on the ground while they examined the bog. Then, arriving at a decision, they withdrew the poles and threw their victim, still bound up in the carpet, into a deep bog-hole. Their next task was to obliterate their footprints, a simple under taking on the edge of a quagmire.

Then Mannering acted. He cut a notch in the fir behind which he was standing, took the exact bearings of the place where the body was hidden, and crept out, jumping the last six feet so as to leave no token of his passage. He was thoroughly screened by the lie of the land. He had only to run a few yards while the ghouls walked two hundred, and they were not yet satisfied with their efforts to conceal the marks which would otherwise be left in the soft ground.

He had gone through a trying ordeal with courage and resource, but he was undeniably shaken, and a half-mile at almost sprinting pace was hardly a sedative. He was just getting a real grip on himself when he saw Betty's car.

It was necessary, of course, in his recital to the girl and the policeman that he should go back to the storm— the boisterous herald of so much adventure. Never had story-teller a more attentive audience. He felt that an almost in credible narrative had been accepted literally, so did not hesitate to recommend the line of action he had decided on during that last vigil in the wood.

The policeman adopted it without demur. He saw the folly of attempting to tackle empty handed a pair of well-armed desperadoes. Indeed, he behaved with exemplary speed and thoroughness. Riding back to the village of Elmdale, where, fortunately, three cars were available, he collected eight stout fellows who possessed and could use 12-bore guns. He despatched a youth on a bicycle to the police superintendent at the nearest market town, six miles away, judging, soundly enough, that a hastily scribbled report would reach headquarters more quickly by that means than by the laborious spelling out of a telegram on an old-fashioned instrument in the village post-office.

Mannering meanwhile, wrote a fairly complete description of the wanted men, and this went with P.C. Paxton's statement. He laid stress on the fact that, while the fellow he heard speaking used idiomatic English, he was, nevertheless, a foreigner, probably a Russian. So expeditiously did all arrangements work that within twenty minutes after the three reached Elmdale four cars were speeding back along the road. Miss Hardacre left her baggage in the policeman's house, so she took Paxton and his bicycle in the dicky.

At the nearest angle of the wood two men alighted, their mission being to take cover behind the shrubs which shut in the garden to the south. Two others dashed on to guard the north end of the bog. The remaining four, having parked the cars in the paddock, accompanied Mannering and the policeman, both being provided with useful weapons, the one with a heavy but serviceable army revolver, and the other with an automatic pistol. This party would undertake the direct attack. Miss Hardacre, of course, was strictly enjoined to remain in her car with her dog, keep the engine running, and, from a safe distance, watch the wood for any attempted breakaway.

The next five minutes were thrilling. The Elmdale farmers were spread out to safeguard the advance of their two leaders, and challenge anyone who appeared at the visible doors or windows. Thus they commanded the house on three sides; the fourth, facing west, was in clear view of each of the outlying groups.

But the thrills were wholly imaginary. The farm was empty. The only real evidence of any prior disturbance was the broken window, furniture, and china. Even the clock had been restored to the mantelpiece and was ticking away merrily. It had stopped at half-past two, and the hands stood now at five minutes to three, so only twenty-five minutes had elapsed since it was picked up and the pendulum started again, probably without the knowledge of the person who put it back in its place.

P.C. Paxton proved to be really efficient. No sooner was he convinced that the birds were flown than he secured three volunteers who would mount to the highest points of the surrounding moors and signal the direction taken by the fugitives if they were sighted. Two were detailed to recover the body from the bog, two posted north and south of the wood, and one upstairs on the west side. Neither of the doors could be opened. They were locked, and both keys were missing.

Within a few minutes the men who had gone to the bog reported their failure to locate the body, so Mannering found his marked tree, and took the exact bearings. He had sent them to the right place in the first instance, but this time he went with them. They, of course, knowing the ways of bogs from which turf had been cut, soon convinced him that a pitch-fork and rake must reveal the presence of such a bulky thing as a human body wrapped in a carpet if it were deposited in six feet of slime and water, while it could not possibly have been thrown from the spot indicated into the next pit of sufficient size for the purpose.

It was not surprising, therefore, that P.C. Paxton began to doubt. His manner changed forthwith. He listened to Mannering's comments without deference, if not with open scepticism. He believed he was being humbugged.

At last, when no news came from any quarter—when the scouts on the hill-tops made no sign, and Paxton was fuming because the superintendent was long overdue—Mannering walked to the gate to have a word with the lady in the car. The policeman went with him—would not let him out of his sight, in fact.

Miss Hardacre was unfeignedly glad to see them.

"Well," she said, "as nothing seems to be happening, may I get out and have a look? I'm tired of sitting here."

"Ask our worthy constable," said Mannering wearily. "Everything has come unstuck. The only definite fact before us at the moment is P.C. Paxton's manifest intent to arrest me if I show the least desire to bolt."

He held out the revolver, holding it by the muzzle.

"Here," he went on, with a wry smile, "you had better carry this, Paxton. It is devilish heavy, but if you take charge of it, the odds will be on your side when you want to 'cuff me. Mind you, I'm annoyed, fed to the teeth, so I may resist, and it would be too bad if this young lady got shot in the scuffle."

What tosh!" said Miss Hardacre. "What utter tosh!"

Paxton's weather-tanned face darkened, which was his only possible way of showing embarrassment. But he was not one to be caught out so easily.

Keep the revolver, sir—you may need it yet," he said. "If you find it heavy, shove it on the back seat of the car for the time being. But you can hardly expect me to pretend that this queer business is working out along the lines of the statements you made at first."

"What's gone wrong?" demanded the girl. "Or, maybe, that's a silly thing to ask? Is Sir William alive and well?"

"You seem to forget that I told you he was dead," snapped Mannering. "He is not only dead but missing. We cannot find his body."

The girl was minded to resent his tone, but thought better of it.

"Of course, we are bound to assume that you are not misleading us wilfully," she said, with a delightfully judicial air which, in other circumstances, would have amused Mannering greatly. "If you really did see him lying dead in the house and his body thrown into the bog soon afterwards, then, if it is not there now, it must have been removed—taken, perhaps along this very road. It certainly did not pass us. How far away is the next village?"

"About five miles, miss," said Paxton.

"I can run one of you there in ten minutes, unless the road surface is too bad. Is there another road on that side of the hill?" and she pointed to the crest beyond the bog.

Mannering looked at her with a new interest, but she evidently preferred to deal with the policeman.

"There's something in what you say, miss," came the ready admission. "The nearest road beyond the hill is two miles away. It joins our road at Elmdale, but you would hardly notice it because it curves round the church, and seems to come in from the south-west."

"Where does it join a main road?"

"Five miles away, just like this one. It runs into the same road, in fact."

"Is it practicable for a car?"

"Oh yes. All these moor tracks are alike. They tell me that once they were the only highways, as the valleys were mostly bogs."

"Well, what about it? Shall we go? And who comes? Both of you?"

"No," said Mannering, rousing himself to take command once more. "Those scoundrels may be in the wood all the time, waiting for a chance to break away. It would not be fair to our friends from the village to put all the responsibility on their shoulders. You go, Paxton. I'll stand fast here."

Obviously the policeman did not know how to act for, the best. "What would you have done?" he asked piteously when discussing his dilemma later with his sergeant, who had expressed the opinion that it might have been wise had he accepted the young lady's offer. "There was no body to be found, an' my orders were to keep an eye on the farm while avoiding the old gentleman. How could I rush off a good five miles, an' leave this chap, who seemed to know all about it, to do as he damn well liked?"

Naturally, he kept his thoughts to himself. He did not even answer Mannering directly.

"If only the superintendent would come!" he growled, turning to scan the undulating road to Elmdale. No speeding car was in sight, but, rising out of the dip on the farther side of which Mannering had halted Betty Hardacre, came a horse and dog-cart at a steady jog-trot.

"Ah!" he went on excitedly, "now we shall get to know something. Here are Freddy Birch and his wife. They keep house for Mr. Hope. To-day is the regular market day at Foxton, though the fair is on this week. Odd I never thought of it. Of course, they've been shopping."

"It will take exactly quarter of an hour to make them begin to understand what has happened," broke in Mannering impatiently. "Then the superintendent will arrive, and another quarter of an hour will be wasted over him. Miss Hardacre has made by far the most sensible suggestion put forward by any of us up to the present moment. Why in the world don't you accept it? I would offer to go myself, but I, a mere stranger, may not be listened to."

A shout reached them from the distant bog.

"By God, those fellows have found something!" cried Paxton, his voice cracking in a falsetto.

He made off, leaping the broken-down fence. At exactly the same place the storm had driven Mannering headlong into an almost fantastic tragedy. Instantly Miss Hardacre bounced out of the car, and the dog sprang after her, yelping joyously.

"For goodness' sake, Tags, shut up!" cried the girl. She turned to Mannering, but hardly looked at him. "I think I have, a sort of right to know what is going on," she announced. "I, at least, can justify my presence, and, in any event, you men seem to be bungling matters between you."

She may have meant to provoke a retort, but Mannering paid no heed, so she followed the policeman across the rough pasture. She was slight of figure and graceful in movement. She ran like one to whom running came naturally. Mannering was by way of being an athlete, so he approved her style.

"The new woman!" he said to himself. "Rather too confident in herself, perhaps, but full of pep and able to use her brains. Well, she could hardly be qualified to assist Sandling other wise. For all that, she has not quite taken my measure yet. She failed to see that I gave her all the credit for a perfectly obvious bit of reasoning. Someone must act. It's up to me, I suppose."

Whereupon he twisted the steering-wheel, pushed the car backward, reversed the operation, and soon had the vehicle facing the way he wanted to go, thus avoiding the noise of backing and turning under power. Then he took the driver's seat and put the engine in gear.

The policeman was bending over a sodden and mire-laden bundle which the two farmers had retrieved from a bog-hole some forty yards nearer the house when he heard the initial clatter of the exhaust. He looked up and turned, to find Miss Hardacre gazing blankly in the direction of the road, which she could not see from this lower level.

"What's that?" he demanded fiercely.

It had just dawned on him that Mannering had not misled him in the least, because the men of their own accord had carried on the search, and soon discovered a place where no effort had been made to conceal the recent presence of more than one person by the bog-side. But they did not proclaim the fact until pitch-fork and rake had brought to land a body rolled in a carpet.

The girl ignored the question. She seemed to be listening intently.

"Can't you speak?" bawled Paxton. "What car is that?"

"Oh, do hold your tongue!" said Miss Hardacre. "You're worse than Tags!"

The unhappy constable wanted badly to make sure of the identity of the man who had been recovered from the bog, but that was impossible until the black slime had been cleared away to some extent. He was equally anxious to know what was happening on the road, and called all his gods to witness that when a woman was a, fool she could be a blithering idiot. Luckily, he expressed his opinions sotto voce, as they still say in musical circles, because the lady explained things most luckily a few seconds later.

"Mr. Mannering has gone off in my car," she said. "It changes gear trickily when it's put into top, but he has managed it all right."

"Gone off? Where's he gone?"

"To do what you refused to do—warn some one miles away down there, where there may be telephones and civilisation."

"Then who is guarding the wood?"

"Oh, he thinks we may have sense enough to attend to that. Perhaps I had better take on my job again. Lend me a gun. I won't shoot anybody with the first barrel. If you hear a shot, come quickly. And I suppose I had better warn Mr. and Mrs. Birch what to expect here. Now, am I to have that gun or not? What an exasperating man you are! You seem to think that everybody wants to get the better of you!"

Paxton choked. He dared not open his mouth, but nodded to one of his helpers, whose 12-bore rested on a small hillock.

"Do you understand the safety catch, miss?" inquired the man civilly.

"Yes, of course. What use would a gun be if I didn't?"

She threw the weapon under her right arm and raced off with the dog.

"By gum!" said the Yorkshireman approvingly; "that young woman's a bit of all right—she is, an' all."

"She doesn't know a damn thing about this business, yet she sticks up for the fellow who has run away with her car!" hissed Paxton.

However, other matters called for his immediate attention. He had seen Sir William Sandling twice during the past three weeks, but the great man himself, while perfectly civil and ready with a cigar and a whisky and soda, did not want to be bothered by the county constabulary. Birch, brought from the village with his wife to take care of the house, had only succeeded in puzzling Paxton by his account of the gentleman's "queer goin's on." It seemed that "Mr. Hope" slept late into the day, breakfasted in his room, ate a hearty meal about seven o'clock, and, weather permitting, would sit or walk by the side of the bog until long after midnight. He never went anywhere else, not even as far as the gate. When rain fell or the wind was strong, he would shut himself up in his sitting-room and read or write, varying this programme by visits to another small room where he kept an extraordinary array of jars and bottles, together with a number of glass cylinders and "decanters" with curiously twisted necks. The Birches were ordered not to go near this room on any account, the almost certain penalty for disobedience being instant death by poison gas or corrosive acid. Probably, if we knew the truth, Bluebeard was an analytical chemist.

But such startling alchemy had not worried Paxton. The mysterious tenant of Blackdown Farm was vouched for by the authorities. The superintendent's orders were specific. Sir William—whose correct name must not be divulged without urgent reason—was not to be kept under any sort of surveillance. In fact, he had better be disregarded altogether unless he sought assistance. In that event, the police would be entirely at his service.

This was all very strange and puzzling, of course, but even the humdrum life of a country policeman is often varied by secret duties of public importance of which no hint ever appears in the newspapers or any printed document.

So Paxton concentrated now on an unpleasant task. He had to clear away sufficient of the peaty mud to make sure that the body was actually that of Sir William Sandling.

Meanwhile, Betty Hardacre had met the Birches. The husband, a powerfully built man of forty, who had lost an eye and three fingers of his left hand and had his left leg badly shattered, all by one shell-burst in the "mushroom trench" at Chapelle d'Armentières in 1916, was opening the gate when the girl crossed the small pasture. He was a pleasant-looking fellow. His wife, some years younger, impressed Betty at once as a capable Yorkshirewoman, who would make light of the duties of a small household. Even the sturdy pony seemed to be a good-natured animal.

Betty was spared the worst part of a painful experience. Some inkling of the truth had reached the couple as they passed through the village.

Birch halted the pony, leaving the gate open.

"Mebbe you'll be Miss Hardacre?" he said in the oblique Yorkshire way, which always avoids a straight question or answer if at all possible.

"Yes," said the girl. "You expected me, of course? I suppose you know already that bad news awaits your return home?"

"Weel, miss" began the man, but his wife yielded to the strain.

"Oh, miss," she cried brokenly, "is it true what we were tellt i' Elmdale? Is t'master dead?"

"I'm afraid it is only too true," said Betty. "I have just seen his body taken from the bog."

"Ah, that nasty bog! Many a time this past three weeks hey' I worrited about t'master fallin' in—isn't that so, Freddy?"

But Birch, as a soldier, knew that men did not hurry off with guns because someone had plunged into a bog-hole.

"Let be, Mollie," he advised gravely. "P'r'aps t'young leddy will tell us what's happened."

"Shall I help you down first, Mrs. Birch?" said Betty, for the poor woman's healthy cheeks had suddenly gone white, and she seemed to have collapsed against the back rail of the seat.

Resting the gun against a gate-post, she assisted Mrs. Birch to alight.

"You must prepare for a great shock," she said gently. "Sir William was killed little more than an hour ago. The police and some of your neighbours are now searching for the men who are supposed to have done this terrible thing."

"Sir William!" bleated the other woman, her dismay yielding to bewilderment at the sound of a strange name.

"Oh, I'm sorry—I mean Mr. Hope. Please try and forget, both of you, that I alluded to him in that way. But, really, I can tell you very little. None of us knows the actual facts. I was stopped on the road, and have not even been inside the house yet. But I do hope you will be brave and helpful. They are carrying in the body now. I believe all the doors are locked, so they will go through the garden. If you care to stop here with me, come into the road, as I am on guard there."

"On guard for what, miss?" broke in Birch.

"For the men—there are two of them. They may be hiding in the wood. We know so little. Everything is blurred and doubtful."

"You come wi' me, Mollie," decided Birch at once. "We'll tie the pony in t'yard an' loosen t'girths. He may be wanted again in a hurry. Then I reckon you'd better find them spare keys an' give 'em to Paxton. . . . Please excuse us, miss. We'll be of more use inside than out."

"One word. You met no one, I suppose, going toward Elmdale?"

"Not a soul, miss. This is a lonely road, especially on a feast-day at Foxton. T'folk are all that side o' t'country."

Betty picked up the gun and went through the gate. She felt that her post had been neglected for a few minutes, and was not quite at ease about it. However, the pair in the dog cart had covered, though unconsciously, the greater part of the interval.

She took her duties seriously now. Not only the road and the wood, but every strip of the surrounding moors in sight was watched intently. After, quarter of an hour of an almost unnerving solitude, she was profoundly glad of the dog's companionship. She could hardly have believed that any wide stretch of land quite so desolate and deserted could exist in England. Even the farm seemed to be devoid of life, though she heard the door inside the porch being unlocked and unbolted. She wondered what they were doing in there, yet was glad that the exigencies of the hour kept her away from the gruesome spectacle which that masterful person, Robert Mannering, had warned her against so tactfully.

This affair abounded in singular, almost phenomenal, features. Why had Sir William Sandling buried himself in such an outlandish spot? It could hardly be for valid scientific research, where he was remote from libraries and laboratories—where even materials for the simplest experiments or tests would be either lacking altogether or extraordinarily difficult to procure. Even the Birchs' dog-cart contained nothing but household stores, which could be diagnosed in their wrappings as so many pounds of flour, bacon, sugar, and the rest. Yet all sorts of people, including Government departments, knew of his whereabouts and were interested in his doings. Why, then, was he not protected? Why was he left utterly alone during so many hours? She had never set eyes on the man, but his international repute stood so high that his love of seclusion, his positive hatred of that public incense so freely offered to high achievement, his refusal to claim credit for the remark able discoveries for which he alone was undoubtedly responsible, were commonplaces among his contemporaries.

She had been packed off to assist him at practically a day's notice, and was made aware that she ought to regard herself as greatly favoured in being chosen for such a position. She was an eminently sensible young woman, and did not flatter herself for a moment that her own success in gaining her London B.Sc. and being appointed to an important post in a North-Country college were the sole qualifications for her new duties, whatever they might be. Rather did she assume that her skill as a typist and shorthand-writer was her real asset, while her training had familiarised her with the jargon of modern science, and she might be trusted to avoid exasperating mistakes when the savant was tabulating his ideas.

Smoke began to curl upwards from the kitchen chimney, and Betty became aware forthwith that she was desperately hungry. It was now well after four o'clock, and she had breakfasted at half-past eight. She had not bothered to lunch on the way, and the storm had intervened. Even then, taking refuge in a farm, she had not thought of asking for food. Now she was eager to chew a hard crust or a rind of bacon!

Tags barked viciously. A man leaped the fence behind Betty, who was so startled that the gun swung into position quickly, with the result that the man was alarmed too.

"It's all right, miss!" he said. "I'm from the village. I came with the party."

Betty hoped he had not noticed her fright. She railed at the terrier and got him pacified.

"Yes," she said. "I recognised you at once, of course. Have you seen anything?"

"A queer kind of blaze away over the moors to the north. If the heather wasn't soakin' wet I'd say it was on fire."

"A blaze? Can it be a house or a rick?"

"There's no house within miles, miss, and no rick. Stacks of peat in plenty—but, after that rain! If you come here, miss, and stand on the wall, you can see it."

Soon Betty was gazing at a column of dense smoke rising above the distant skyline. Already it was spreading out at the top in a far-flung canopy.

"That must be a long way off," she said.

"Best part of eight miles by road, miss."

"Is there a road in that direction?"

"Yes. The Whitby and Guisborough high road runs along the far side of the hill, and every village in Eskdale has a side road to it. They're mostly a couple of miles long."

"Hadn't you better tell the policeman? Then he may send some of you after Mr. Mannering, who has taken my car. That fire strikes me as a sort of signal. As you say, the heather cannot possibly burn to-day, though at this time of the year there must be people roaming about in all directions."

"Not so soon after that storm, miss. And we'll have another before we're much older."

Betty remembered that a small cloud had appeared in the south-west some minutes earlier. She looked now, and saw that it was much larger and travelling swiftly, though the breeze sweeping across the moor just then barely stirred the highest fronds of the firs.

But a speeding open car coming from Elmdale was of more immediate interest. Her farmer friend was scrutinising it too.

"That'll be Superintendent Dunkeld, frae Foxton," he said. "Now we'll all get our marchin' orders. He's sharp is Mr. Dunkeld. He'll know what to do, an' no mistake."

Betty leaped down from the wall, retrieving her gun, which she had placed in safety before climbing on to a not too firm perch.

The car stopped in front of the gate. A somewhat slightly built man in a braided uniform got out, leaving a sergeant and two constables still seated.

"Are you Miss Hardacre?" he said pleasantly.

"Yes," said Betty, who could not help smiling. "That is the first question nearly every one puts, though I have never before been within fifty miles of this locality."

"The explanation is quite simple," said the superintendent. "We were told you were coming from Leeds to-day. Where is Paxton?"

"In the farm."

"And why are you remaining here?"

"I'm a sentry, of sorts."

"Guarding what?"

"The wood. Mr. Mannering thinks there is a chance that the men who killed—Mr. Hope—may still be hiding there."

"Ah, Mr. Mannering—who discovered the crime. Where is he?"

"Gone off in my car."

"Indeed. Where to?"

"That way "—and Betty pointed north. "The men have escaped," she added. "He believed—and I agreed with him—that some inquiry should be started along that line. I really don't know what he means to do. He hurried off just as your policeman and some others found the body in the bog."

The superintendent drew a slip of paper from a pocket-book and gave it to one of the constables, bidding him take Miss Hardacre's place and detain anyone who resembled the men described on the paper, which was Mannering's memorandum. The chauffeur was to stand fast with the car.

"Remember," he said, "that the fellows we are looking for are armed, so have your own automatics ready."

He was surprised at finding three cars lined up in the field near the outbuildings.

"My word!" he said. "Paxton soon got a force together; but why have not two of those cars, at least, begun to scour the country?"

"They just couldn't," explained Betty. "There wasn't a man to spare. This place had to be surrounded. I really don't think much time has been lost. Everything is so puzzling."

Though ready enough to twit both Mannering and the policeman to their faces, she would hear nothing said against them in their absence.

Mr. Dunkeld did not pursue the point.

"And you, Mr. Trenholme?" he said to the farmer. "What is your special job?"

Trenholme told of the pillar of smoke seen from the hill-top.

"Ah!" came the comment. "Come along, Miss Hardacre. We'll go to the house."

In a lower voice, when they were not likely to be overheard, he added: "This is an extraordinary crime. Unless we are lucky, it will not be cleared up straight away. Scotland Yard takes a most serious view of it. Two of their best men have started from London already, and will be at my place in Foxton about ten o'clock to-night. Of course, we'll do what we can here and now. I hope Mr. Mannering comes back soon. He seems to be a useful sort of person."

"Oh, he is!" agreed Betty. "He certainly surprised me from the very beginning, and I'm afraid I ticked him off."

"Ticked him off! Why?"

"He made me do just what he wanted. Stupid of me, of course, but I'm not accustomed to being treated as a nonentity. . . . Please don't tell him I said that."

"No fear," said the superintendent, with a gravity which Betty was inclined to suspect. "I shall have enough on my hands during the next few hours without starting a row between you and Mr. Mannering."

Betty flushed a little, but repressed the words on her lips.

"What I really want to know now is the meaning of that column of smoke away to the north," went on Dunkeld. "We saw it, too, from the last rise in the road. I think I shall have to send my own car there at once, but first I must hear what Paxton has to say."

CHAPTER 3: WHAT BETTY DISCOVERED

"Do you think it will sound quite heartless if I ask Mrs. Birch to make me a cup of tea?" said Betty. "I have an aching void where my lunch ought to be. If I don't eat something soon I shall fade right out of the picture."

"The very thing," agreed the superintendent with a sudden geniality that was almost surprising. "We can't have you put out of action, because I want you to take charge here."

"Take charge? In what way?"

"There's heaps of things to be done. For instance, some expert qualified for the task should collect Sir William's papers and see that they are put under lock and key, separating the purely scientific ones from those of a personal nature, if any. Then we must discover his relatives and communicate with them. A doctor will be here at any moment now. When I have his opinion as to the exact cause of death, I have to consider the time and place for the inquest. But I shall leave many details in your capable hands. And why not? You are Sir William's secretary. Wait here a few seconds till I find Mrs. Birch."

They were standing in the porch now, and Mr. Dunkeld's hand was on the latch, but Betty caught his arm.

"Don't think it foolish of me," she said, "but—will you—make sure that it is really Sir William Sandling who has been deprived of life so suddenly? I—I can hardly bring myself to believe it."

"Is there any doubt in the matter?"

"I don't know. I have not yet heard that your policeman or Mr. Birch, who could not be mistaken about it, has identified him."

"Oh, I see. I was under the impression that Mr. Mannering's evidence was quite clear on the point. However, I'll come back without delay."

He was good as his word. Betty had hardly envisioned the new and grave duties which had been thrust on her so unexpectedly before the door opened and the superintendent beckoned her in. Tags grew excited instantly, so his mistress carried him.

"Mrs. Birch will look after you in the kitchen," said her guide. "It lies that way, to the right. The passage is rather dark, but the kitchen door is open. And I am sorry to say that I, as well as others, have recognised Sir William. It's a sad business, and we can only make the best of it. By the way, I am sending a sergeant and a constable after Mr. Mannering. A heavy shower is approaching, so they will start as soon as the car has its hood up."

Betty reflected ruefully that her own car might suffer, because a driver not acquainted with its gadgets might be unable to protect it quickly enough if caught in the open country. However, she said nothing. She almost felt ashamed of thinking about such trivialities. It did not occur to her that the normal mind may be likened to a cup which, if filled to overflowing, not only can, hold no more, but actually loses some of its contents. Not yet could she measure the extent of the strange experiences of the past hour. Later, reviewing them in detail, she marvelled at her own endurance. Her twenty-three years of life had been placid, but fully occupied. Now she had been plunged into stormy waters.

She found Mrs. Birch frying ham and cutting bread and butter in piles. A kettle was nearly a-boil, eggs were in readiness to be cracked and popped into the pan, and the table was spread with cups and saucers, pastries, and a currant loaf. Betty was almost moved to protest, until she remembered suddenly how someone had told her once that if the Last Day were fixed irrevocably for six o'clock p.m. on a given date, Yorkshire would still have its "high tea" at five.

"Can I help?" she said. "If you want any more bread and butter, I can do that all right, and make the tea as well."

"Nay, honey," came the cheery answer. "I can manage, unless you'd like te warm t'tea-pot, an' put in half a cupful o' tea out o' that canister on t'shelf. Then you an' me can have a bite, as the men will be wantin' theirs. It's a fair relief to be busy—it is, an' all. I didn't think I could do a thing till I started. But, there! Don't let's talk about what has happened. Worritin' is nëa use. What's dëan is dëan, an' that's all there is tiv it!"

Betty was well aware that the county of broad acres changes its speech from fairly good English to the vernacular with a suddenness that often leaves the Southerner gasping. But she appreciated Mrs. Birch's philosophy, and acted on it. Moreover, the sizzling of the first egg had a peculiarly grateful and comforting sound. It calmed the dog, too. For the first time since she entered the house, Betty was able to relax her grip on his collar.

The kitchen darkened, and the rain came on in fierce gusts. A car roared away, and another arrived—her own, as she could tell by the beat of the engine.

She had just got through a well-filled plate, and was therefore all the more able to enjoy her tea, when Mr. Dunkeld came in, piloting a tall, thin man who might have had his profession branded on a care-lined forehead.

"Dr. Lysaght and I are in the same case as you, Miss Hardacre," he said with a seriousness which Betty was beginning to regard as a veneer nicely adjusted to conceal an ever-present sense of humour. "It is always the way. Let a doctor or a policeman miss a meal, and Fate generally arranges that he shall be deprived of the next one. However, we are lucky this time. Now, Mrs. Birch, don't you dare move. We can help ourselves, and we have to make way for others, you know. . . . No news of your friend yet, Miss Hardacre."

"Meaning Mr. Mannering?" she retorted.

"Well, yes. I bracket you two together. At any rate, he isn't an enemy. Paxton tells me he is a first-rate organiser—got things going like clockwork along the right lines."

Betty swallowed a bit of ham without giving it anything like the orthodox twenty-nine bites.

"I think so highly of him that when he brings back my car half full of water I shall want to forgive him," she said.

"Where are you people all going to stay to night?" put in the doctor. "I've been hearing about you from the superintendent Miss Hardacre, and my wife will find you a room. We can put up Mr. Mannering as well if he has made no other arrangements. Foxton inns are all full. We are bang in the middle of our annual three days' fair and feast."

"I understand he is on a walking tour," said Betty. "As for myself, I am greatly obliged to you. Of course, there's a bedroom here for me, but candidly—"

"Not to be thought of," decreed Dunkeld firmly. "That's all right, Mrs. Birch. You and your husband will be well looked after. I shall leave three constables here all night, and two will be on guard together. . . . Now, is everything settled? Let us eat with enthusiasm for five minutes. Then, when the shower passes, we three can have a conference in the open air."

It was really quite pleasant, reflected Betty, to have one's difficulties solved before one said a word. Hitherto she had been accustomed to the academic method, which stated a thesis, analysed it fully and more or less logically, and often arrived at a decision which pleased nobody. Here was a practical man who knew exactly what to do and saw that others did it, too, yet seemed to have the knack of setting people at their ease by meeting their wishes.

"I hate to suggest anything which might break in on our present occupation," commented Dr. Lysaght, "but we are a long way from every where in terms of telegrams and telephones. How would it be if we considered the best means of getting in touch with Sir William's relatives? Then we could make a start by sending a man to Foxton. Elmdale is simply hopeless."

"That has been done," said Dunkeld. "Scot land Yard has promised full information. A motor cyclist may bring it here any minute. Another egg, doctor?"

"Thanks. You're wasted in Foxton, superintendent. Why in the world don't you shift to one of the big centres, if not to the Yard itself?"

"Because, in Foxton, I have some valued friends. My doctor, the magistrate's clerk, the chairman of the Bench, are all excellent fellows. They allow for my weaknesses and I appreciate their fine qualities. Why should I want to leave them?"

"After that little speech you will understand, Miss Hardacre, the well-deserved popularity of our chief of police," said Lysaght.

"Are you married, Mr. Dunkeld?" inquired Betty.

The superintendent laughed quietly.

"Trust a woman to ferret out the real reason for my devotion to Foxton," he said. "My wife loves the little town. I retire on a pension in two years' time, and we have bought our house already. Why, only the other day the doctor here persuaded me to join the golf club and take lessons in bridge."

"I don't object to an occasional discussion about an interesting hand at auction," said Lysaght, "but I give you fair warning that I shall not endure a full and detailed description of how you once did the dog-leg hole in three."

Most of this chatter might have been in Choctaw where Mrs. Birch was concerned, but it was quite evident she disapproved of its flippancy. The doctor, happening to notice her set expression, tried to put matters right.

"Are these your famous cheese-cakes?" he asked. "I've often heard of them, but have never before had the chance of eating one."

"Is that so, doctor?" she said dryly. "I was wunnering if ye thowt they were apple tarts. You fine folk are all alike. Yon poor gentleman laid i' t'front room nivver knew nor cared what he was atin'."

"You're mistaken, Mrs. Birch," said the superintendent solemnly. "He wrote and thanked me for having procured a most capable cook. He was delighted with you and your husband."

A corner of her apron was lifted hurriedly to Mrs. Birch's eyes.

"An' to think that Freddy an' me should ha' bin miles away in Foxton, to-day of all days," she sobbed.

"I saw it coming," explained Lysaght when the three were alone in the porch, for the second shower, though lighter, was a persistent one. "We headed her off valiantly for a time, but the break was already overdue."

"Why, before you came in she actually stopped me from talking about Sir William," said Betty.

"Oh, she would, dear soul! You see, we were supposed to sit and eat in solemn silence, broken only by an occasional sigh. She makes no allowance for the other side of life. To-day, for instance, I have removed an adhesive appendix, extracted three teeth, visited a score of bedridden people, and must be in my surgery at 6.30 for a dozen or more panel patients. And the worst job of the lot has been this one. The men who attacked Sir William must have been homicidal maniacs. Well, I can do nothing more at the moment, Dunkeld. . . . Are you and Tags coming with me, Miss Hardacre?"

"No, doctor," broke in the superintendent. "She is wanted here for another hour or so. I have decided to leave the sitting-room exactly as it is till the Scotland Yard men see it early to-morrow, but Miss Hardacre can help by sorting out a lot of papers in Sir William's bedroom. It seems he dealt with all his correspondence there. I'll bring her to your place about half-past seven, if that is a convenient time."

"Splendid. We have supper at eight. Will you join us?"

"If possible. But I don't know yet where I may be at that hour."

"Why? It won't do a ha'porth of good to go tearing round the country."

"I have an idea that Mr. Mannering may cause developments. There is something in the wind, or he would have returned from Duneham long ago. I gave him twenty-five minutes. He has been gone at least fifty."

"Well, bring him, too, if things pan out that way."

A policeman dashed up on a motor-cycle.

"Wait one minute, doctor, and hear what London says," and the superintendent opened a telegram. It read: "Only known relatives a son in horse gunners at Lucknow and married daughter in Kenya Colony. Do not communicate Welbeck Street. Use every effort prevent news papers ascertaining identity to-night. Winter and Furneaux will explain.—SHELDON."

"That's odd," he commented. "Why should we shut down on Welbeck Street?"

"I remember now," said Betty. "Sir William lives there."

"Exactly. We have to avoid the one place one would naturally communicate with."

"The area is beginning to widen," said Lysaght. "London, India, East Africa. Can I do anything for you as to the Press?"

"I've seen to that. The schoolmaster at Elmdale is a local journalist. I told him all about the death of an eccentric old gentleman who was living in seclusion in the depths of the moors. I'll call on him again on the way home. I question if the news agencies will know anything about Sir William Sandling's death by this time to-morrow, as his correct name will not come out at the preliminary inquest. Will three o'clock suit you, doctor?"

"No hour better. I hate to go, but I really must be off. See you all later, I hope."

The superintendent watched Lysaght's car until it turned through the gate.

"Winter and Furneaux," he mused aloud. "The Chief Superintendent of the C.I.D. and his best-known aide. This is a big thing, Miss Hardacre. Do you mind tackling the letters in the bedroom now? Put together everything affecting Welbeck Street—documents bearing that address, I mean. I leave any other rough classification to you. Shall I show you the way? Will you be nervous? You have your dog for company. The house is full of men who will hear if you call, and I shall be in the room beneath."

"Where the body is?"

"Yes. Do you mind?"

"Why should I? But it won't be necessary that I should see it later?"

"That is the one thing I am anxious you should avoid, I assure you."

Betty found herself in a pleasant, low-ceilinged room with two windows facing south. They were open, and the scent of mignonette was surprising and most agreeable. The sun was breaking through again, so the beauty of the garden was enhanced by the diamond raindrops on every leaf and flower. She was just as astonished as Mannering had been by the contrast between the trim lawn with its radiant flower-beds and the tangled wilderness in front of the house. It was odd how everything connected with Blackdown Farm savoured now of mystery, whereas only a few hours earlier it was as peaceful a spot as could be found in any part of rural England.

Tags had to be spoken to severely before he would settle down. He knew quite well that there was something wrong somewhere. He was restless, and wanted to whine. As his lead was behind a cushion in the car, Betty looked around for a piece of rope or something of the sort which might act as a makeshift for the hour, and this simple incident led at once to a real discovery. A long, thin strap—the very thing she wanted—was coiled up on a strongly made box. It was actually in her hand when she noticed that the lock had been forced with great violence.

Naturally, she lifted the lid, and saw that the contents, nearly all textbooks dealing with gases and coal-tar extracts, had been tumbled about roughly. There was every evidence of a frenzied search for something. Whether the object sought for had been extracted it was impossible to determine, but the immediate problem was offered by the strap. Presumably, Sir William's assailants had ransacked the room; even so, why had they troubled to replace something which must have fallen off the box the instant it was opened?

The strap was a new one, of good quality, and had never been used; it was actually tied with a small label bearing the name of a Newcastle saddler. Somehow Betty sensed that this was an important find.

Now she had a closer eye for the books, and it was just her scientific training which led her to single out one volume from about forty others, because it had an old binding and was entitled "The Arch of Sussex," a most remark able companion for such books as "Producer Gas and Gas Producers," by Wyer, Frier and West's "Chemical Warfare, 1921," and Meyer's "Der Gaskampf und die Chemischen Kampfstoffe."

It was tucked into a corner of the box, and had not been disturbed because there could be nothing beneath it. Yet Betty picked it up, and was instantly aware that it was not a book at all, but a dummy. Taking it to the window she made out a well-worn patch in the leather and pressed it. The "book" opened easily. She took out a considerable sum of money in notes—over £200 when it was counted—and a locked diary.

"Well, that's a good start, anyhow," she mused. "Knowing what I do, and guessing a good deal, I should not be surprised if I were told that the diary was what those scoundrels wanted, much more than the money."

This theory was largely borne out by her subsequent investigations. Every drawer in a dressing-table and writing-desk had been rummaged. A gold watch and gold match-box, with a platinum and diamond chain such as men wear when in evening dress, some pearl studs, and a few pounds' worth of silver coins had not been taken, whereas every shirt and collar fresh from the laundry had been thrust all ways in a frenzied effort to find something in a great hurry. Again Betty glanced at the diary. She wished she could look inside, but that must wait until she was authorised to break open the lock or find a key to fit it.

Then she busied herself with the papers in the writing-desk. There were a great many, tumbled about in utmost disorder. Giving each the barest scrutiny, she soon evolved a rough system of dividing them into batches. She singled out one letter which, she thought, Mr. Dunkeld might like to see very soon. It was dated from Welbeck Street about fourteen days earlier, and had been sent to a bank in York, whence it was re-addressed in a new envelope to "William Hope, Esq., care of the Postmaster, Foxton," which, by the way, was the address borne by Sir William's letter to her. It ran

"DEAR SIR WILLIAM,

"While I am sure you have the best of reasons for keeping your present whereabouts hidden, I have to point out that my position is rendered thereby more than a trifle awkward. Professor Vorhinoff called to-day, and was exceedingly annoyed when told he would have to communicate with you through a Yorkshire bank. He refused to believe that I had no other address, and reached you myself in that way. At last I persuaded him to write the enclosed note, though he kept on fuming about the delay, saying he would not be answerable for the consequences. His vague hints were alarming enough to one who could not possibly know what he meant, especially as his comments were mainly in Russian.

"I am, yours faithfully,

"BEATRICE BINGHAM."

"A secretary, I suppose?" mused Betty. "Rather an uppish lady, I should imagine, and not altogether trustworthy. Perhaps that is what the Scotland Yard telegram implied. Well, well—I certainly am getting myself bound up with a real mystery!"

She worked on, paying no heed to outside sounds, which were blurred to indistinctness on this side of the house, until she heard footsteps on the stairs. Meanwhile, she had not come across anything which seemed to be the note referred to in the letter.

Tags barked, of course, but not aggressively. He knew already that the superintendent was free to come and go as he chose.

A taller man entered with Dunkeld. It was Mannering.

"I hear you are prepared to condone the theft of your car, Miss Hardacre," he said, with a pleasant smile. "Let me reassure you at once—it is dry as a bone, whereas I am soaked to the skin. Fortunately, I left it in a stable during the shower, while a policeman took me on his motor bike to investigate the fire among the heather which you saw some time ago.

"What caused it?" she asked.

"So far as we could make out, some clothing and the number-plate of a car were covered with petrol and burnt by the roadside in a lonely part of the moor. Still, it is difficult to destroy anything completely. The policeman and I found some metal buttons bearing the address of a Newcastle-on-Tyne tailor, and a pocket-knife with the name of a German maker stamped on the blades."

"Newcastle!" cried Betty. "Look at this, then!" and she produced the strap.

She said nothing, however, as to her other exhibits until Mannering had excused himself, as he wanted to change his clothing.

The superintendent was immensely impressed by the Welbeck Street letter and the diary.

"You had better safeguard the money," he said. "You will be called on to spend a good deal of it during the next few days. And now, when Mr. Mannering is ready, I'll pilot both of you to Foxton. It is growing late. We can do nothing more here to-night. To-morrow, if my colleagues of the C. I. D. approve, you can carry on and finish your job thoroughly, though that does not imply any failure on your part to accomplish a tremendous lot already. Between you and Mr. Mannering I shall be kept busy on the phone for hours, because several lines of inquiry are opening up, so I cannot join you at the doctor's house."

"Did the men escape in a car?" she could not help asking.

"Yes, but that second heavy shower obliterated all wheel-marks, so pursuit over the moor was hopeless. Mannering and the policeman pushed on as far as the main road. Then they did not even know which way to turn, so Mr. Mannering elected to come back here in your car, while the local constable and the other men I sent to Duneham are trying to find someone who saw the suspected car while it was on the cross-country track. They may secure a description, but I doubt it. We have had some share of luck already, and we cannot expect too much. This affair was well planned. If it failed in its main object it was not because of any blunder by the men who killed Sir William. Of course, we do not know yet how far they really succeeded. I don't think they came here to commit murder. They sought something vastly more important than the life of any one individual. But, there I am only guessing, a bad habit in a dry-as-dust policeman. . . . Come along! Leave the room just as it is. It will not be disturbed to-night."

Chapter 4: The C.I.D. in Action

SUPERINTENDENT DUNKELD, being a bit of a philosopher, had uttered no word of complaint when he heard from Mannering the story of the burnt clothing on High Riggs Moor. It was not his fault that there was no telephone in the police-station at Duneham; otherwise the heavy gates of a railway crossing in that village might have blocked the path of the escaping criminals. He did his best by instructing the inspector he left in charge at Foxton to get on the phone to every county town lying north of Blackdown Farm, and give the local police Mannering's written description of the wanted men.

Indeed, he made light of his difficulties in subsequent discussion of the hazards of the hour.

"I believe now," he would say solemnly, though his eyes would be smiling, "that the absence of a phone at Duneham saved the life of the constable stationed there. Those fellows would have shot him at sight. While high powered cars are used by scoundrels who know that their capture means being hanged in due process of law, they will not surrender merely because a policeman holds up his hand. The only way we can deal with the murderer or burglar with a speedy car at his disposal is to place strong steel gates across all key roads, and a lot more people will have to be killed before the free born Briton will submit to a whole countryside being closed to traffic for many hours while the police examine every vehicle which tries to pass."

Probably he was right in both respects. The good fortune of the Duneham man was almost demonstrable, yet the great British public would certainly howl with indignation if transit were unduly delayed because of an attempt to arrest a fugitive who, when he knew he could not break through the cordon on wheels, would endeavour to dodge it on foot.

But the superintendent's genuine grievance was the destruction of the clothes which might have led to the two men being seen and identified almost anywhere in the North of England. The Newcastle saddler who had sold the strap found by Betty recognised Mannering's description of the men, while the ready-made clothing house which had supplied the two suits were equally helpful. These purchases had been made the previous afternoon. The car was the real stumbling block. No one had seen it. Its make, type, and power were quite unknown.

"They were an intelligent pair—there can be no doubt about that," he admitted. "That the leopards should change their spots so promptly was the cleverest trick I have heard of for many a day. And they took no chances at all. If their garments were bloodstained the evidence went up in flame. The burning of the car's number-plate was nothing more than an attempt to mislead the police. They knew, of course, that the metal could not be destroyed in that sort of fire, but it had served its purpose, and might as well be thrown aside there as elsewhere. It bore a number registered in the name of a perfectly respectable citizen of Birmingham, who grew very angry when questioned as to his whereabouts on the afternoon of Tuesday, August 5, but ultimately proved that he was playing golf at Edgbaston, though supposed to be visiting Wolverhampton on business."

In its way, too, it was a slight but queer coincidence that Mannering should have been compelled to substitute a dry suit for his wet one. The rucksack contained just what he needed, and no more. But the rig was much smarter than his pedestrian outfit. He was dressed now for the town rather than the country, which, of course, was merely typical of his unassuming ways, because white linen, blue serge, and black shoes would be far less noticeable in a hotel or restaurant than the open flannel shirt, rough tweeds, and heavy brogues of the open road.

Betty Hardacre noted with approval that he did not seem to care at all if Tag's free gift of hair from neck and back were distributed liberally over a large section of his coat. At any rate, this masterful man was a dog-lover, and she liked him for it.

Dunkeld was good as his word. While Mannering retrieved Betty's baggage from the policeman's cottage at Elmdale, the superintendent gave the local scribe some interesting paragraphs for the newspapers. Then he led the way to Foxton, told the others how to reach the doctor's house, and promised to call early next morning if, as he believed, his time were fully occupied that night.

Mrs. Lysaght made them welcome. She was a bright little woman, and accompanied nearly every sentence with a cheery laugh. It was a mere habit, probably due to nervousness, but it had an oddly embarrassing effect at first.

Her greeting, for instance: "Oh, I'm so glad you got away in good time. Ha-ha! We have rabbit-pie for supper. He-he! And it soon spoils if kept in the oven. Ha-ha!"

"I hope it's a large pie," said Mannering promptly. "My last meal was a bit of bread and cheese and a glass of beer at noon."

"And you, Miss Hardacre? He-he! Aren't you famished? Ha-ha! What a dreadful experience you two had on the moor! He-he!"

Betty gurgled something about Mrs. Birch's "high tea." Her nerves had withstood many assaults that day, but Mrs. Lysaght's giggle tested them almost to the breaking point of hysteria.

The two were shown to their rooms. As Mannering passed Betty's door he muttered: "Didn't you want to whoop, 'Ho-ho!'? I did."

She was grateful to him for saying that. It showed that he sympathised.

However, the lady was an excellent hostess, and her guests soon learnt to ignore a quaint mannerism. The doctor helped them to avoid a long discussion of the murder. In fact, he decided that a good night's rest would be Betty's best tonic, so she was packed off to bed at a comparatively early hour.

Then, while the men smoked the pipe of peace, Lysaght grew confidential.

"Are you an Indian Civil Servant?" he asked, by way of clearing the ground.

"Not in the accepted meaning of the term," said the other. "I was attached to the Political Department out there for some years. I was born in India, and learnt the hill dialect of the Assam coolies when quite a kiddie. Oddly enough, I never forget it, which is contrary to the usual run of things, so, when soldiering took me East again at the end of the war, I drifted somehow into the Secret Service, because Chinese Bolshevists were busy all along the Thibetan frontier."

"Well, I was only being cautious. You see, without actually knowing the facts, I'm sure to day's crime goes far beyond the range of what one may call an ordinary robbery with murder thrown in. In the first place, a lot of people high up in Whitehall were keen on 'Mr. Hope' being given every kind of assistance. Have you been told who 'Mr. Hope' really was?"

"Yes. Indeed, I know now that I ought to have recognised him. I did something of the sort, but subconsciously. It is over twelve years since we met, and I was only a boy of twenty then, so it is nothing to be surprised at if I failed to associate the battered and blood-stained old man at the farm with a famous lecturer on chemistry at Oxford, to whom, in my spare time, I acted as a humble assistant."

"You don't say! In his gas experiments?"

"Yes and no. Before the Boche used chlorine at Langemark in 1915 no human being dreamed of trying poison gas in the war. But 'Hope,' as I think we ought to continue alluding to him, was great on what he used to call basic gases. Remember, the whole universe is made up of them. So, when the first gas attack was launched by the Germans against the French and Canadians, he was one of the few men we could turn to for a reply. But that was long after I had joined up."

"By Jove! This is most interesting. It fits in exactly with certain things which came to my knowledge—hints dropped by various people who hadn't the least idea what they were really talking about—Freddy Birch, for instance, who is a patient of mine. I can guess now what our friend was after. He was studying marsh gas, will-o'-the-wisp, famous in song and story."

"But that is rather astounding, too," said Mannering, leaning forward and looking at Lysaght intently. "Marsh gas, you say? Why, I believe I put him on the track of it."

"How?"

"While I was at Harrow my father, who was a tea-planter, came home—retired, through ill health. During the Long Vac in 1910 he took a bit of shooting at a place called Hipswell, near Richmond, in this Riding. Only six days ago I was staying in the very inn where we lodged. I even stood in the butt where I shot my first grouse. Well, one night in August we remained rather late at a friend's house, and, about midnight, discovered that the magneto of our car was out of action. Motors were not very reliable at that date, you know. We made nothing of a four miles' walk, however, so started home across the moor. There was hardly a house the whole way, but the road was straight and level, and a full moon shone behind scattered clouds. Still, it was light and clear, and we could see a long way in any direction. The road was partly fenced, with stunted trees at intervals. My father was smoking a pipe, and I was explaining the action of a new army rifle which I had seen illustrated in some weekly paper. To make things plain, I was demonstrating the self-loading mechanism on my stick. I mention this trivial incident to show that we were not in a frame of mind to accept any happening as supernatural or savouring of witch-craft. Well, with a suddenness that can only be described as instantaneous, we were surrounded by a mass of blue flame, which seemed to shoot upward with a hiss, leaving us in utter darkness or a few seconds. We each thought that some one had fired a gun from behind a low hedge, but the absence of any report dispelled that notion before it could be expressed even by a word. We were undeniably startled, but calm enough, and searched the open moor on both sides of the road. There was absolutely nothing to account for that rush of flame. Then my father suggested that a collection of marsh gas had drifted into the road from a bog-hole, and that his pipe had ignited it. That is as far as we ever got in theory, or any other way. I remember telling—Mr. Hope—about it, and he was greatly taken by the story. Indeed, he said – "

"Go on! Don't stop now, for goodness' sake!" cried the doctor.

"I suppose there's no harm in repeating his words," though the speaker seemed to be a trifle dubious in the matter. "He said: 'What a tremendous yet devilish thing it would be, Bob, if one could flood a whole country with an impalpable gas of that kind, and then set fire to it. The resultant blaze would blot out a nation, eh?' The absurdity amused me at the time. It doesn't now."

"Because the chemists are nearing some amazing discovery of the sort?"

"I fear so."

"Well, now for the sequel to your yarn. Hope did come here to study marsh gas. I guessed as much a week back. I am certain of it to-night."

"Probably you are right. He was searching for primary causes. Anyone with his technical skill could dispense with laboratories and analyses until he knew exactly what he wanted to produce in quantity."

"But he was not so bare of equipment as you seem to imagine. Didn't you peep into his experimental room?"

"I was not aware such a place existed in the farm."

"That's odd," said Lysaght.

He paused, rather confusedly, so Mannering's next question was almost inevitable. "Does Dunkeld believe I roamed all over the house?"

The other man squirmed quite candidly this time.

"It is only fair to him that we should remember he has not yet heard your account of what occurred soon after three o'clock this afternoon. He accepts Paxton's version for the time being."

"And Paxton, of course, is convinced even now that I have not told him half what I know?" broke in Mannering.

At that the doctor pulled himself together.

"Don't imagine, from anything I have said, that Dunkeld is suspicious where you are concerned," was his emphatic disclaimer. "He spoke about that very matter to me, and said he would ask you to put in writing to-morrow morning every little incident you can recall, every impression, even the fleeting ideas you may have formed and abandoned. He's shrewd and decisive is Dunkeld. He had secured the vital facts which he is broadcasting at this minute, and left the rest to the more settled atmosphere of the morning hours. Then he will probably coach you as to what he wants you to say and what to suppress at the inquest—a purely formal affair in so far as the day's proceedings go. You know, I suppose, that the C.I.D. is sending two of its best men here to-night?"

"Didn't Miss Hardacre tell you?"

"Not a word, though I realise now that Dunkeld hinted at some such development."

Then Mannering rose, and added with a smile

"Take my tip, doctor, and don't you tell me, either. When the authorities give me their confidence, I'll reciprocate. In the meantime I shall be content to figure as a quite commonplace witness, who simply blundered into connection with a crime of which he does not understand the why and wherefore."

Lysaght looked tired and perplexed as he went upstairs. "This is a queer business, and no mistake," he confided to his better half in the privacy of their bedroom.

"He-he! Are Mr. Mannering and Miss Hardacre old friends?" she inquired surprisingly.

"No. They met for the first time on the moore this afternoon."

"Ha-ha! How odd!"

"Why 'odd'?"

"He-he! Did you ever see a better matched couple, Arthur?"

"Oh, for goodness' sake!" growled the doctor.

At breakfast the whole four scanned such morning papers as were available.

"The reporters don't seem to have heard all about you two. Ha-ha!" commented Mrs ysaght.

"I'm glad of that," said Betty instantly.

"Yet fancy their missing the romantic side of, the tragedy! He-he! But they'll get hold of it soon. Ha-hat"

"Now, listen to me, little Bright-Eyes!" snapped her husband. "Let us eat our breakfast in peace. We'll be fed to the teeth with the whole wretched affair before the day is out."

Mrs. Lysaght was not so frivolous as her incessant merriment might seem to indicate. Being a doctor's wife, she knew when she was being told to stop talking. But her obedience was altogether relative. It did not preclude other topics of conversation.

"I do hope you both like Yorkshire bacon. Ha-ha!" she burbled. "Some people don't. He-he. They find it too rich. Ha-ha."

"We never get it in Leeds," ventured Betty. "I was beginning to believe that no such thing existed."

"It does not exist, commercially," explained the doctor. "You would not be eating it now if my fees were not paid in kind occasionally. In that way alone can I secure a properly cured side or a ripe ham."

A maid came in.

"The superintendent has just rung up, sir," she said, "and please will you and the lady and gentleman come round to the White Horse as soon as possible? He didn't wait for an answer."

Lysaght glanced at his watch.

"A quarter to nine," he grumbled, "and my surgery will be full at nine. . . . Get hold of Mr. Dunkeld, Mary, and tell him that, although I may be detained for some time, the others will be there in a few minutes."

"I really ought to have an assistant," he went on, "but what between taxation and the increased prices of everything, even pot. brom; and suiph. mag., I can't afford the extra expense."

"Do you think I may take Tags with me?" mused Betty aloud.

"Why not? This is a sort of preliminary consultation, and Tags is in the affair up to his ears already," put in Mannering quickly. He saw that Mrs. Lysaght was going to say something, and he was beginning to dread her cheery comments.

Foxton was a compact little market town. Usually at that hour of an August day its inhabitants were too busy to be loitering in the one main street. But this Wednesday was the last of three days of combined fair and feast—the latter an old-time festivity rapidly dying out in all but the more remote parts of the Yorkshire dales. Though shorn of much of its gaiety—though the half of one small field more than sufficed for the travelling shows, roundabouts, and swings which in an earlier generation would have filled a couple of acres—though barely a dozen stalls stood where once fifty jostled each other for space in the street—there were still some hundreds of people in evidence.

The White Horse Inn was not more than five minutes' walk from the doctor's residence, but Tags had a hectic passage, because scores of dogs of every possible size and breed deemed this a lawful occasion, and every cur among them resented the presence of a stranger. So Betty had to carry him, while he snarled defiance at all and sundry, with the result that she could hardly exchange a word with her companion. She regretted this. He was so frank with her during their brief meetings of yesterday that she thought she had been rather mean in not confiding to him the happenings at Blackdown Farm during his absence. She had missed a good opportunity while bringing him to Foxton, but her excuse was that the superintendent might not wish her to discuss Sir William's letters and diary. Now that they were all coming face to face, and in the presence of two awesome detectives from Scotland Yard, she had a feeling of unease because of her reticence.

"I am so sorry we have not been able to have a quiet chat this morning," she managed to blurt out during a calm interlude secured by cuffing Tags. "I have so much to say—"

"Of course. But—don't say it. The police will do all the talking necessary. Unless I am greatly mistaken, Miss Hardacre, they know many things which may not be revealed, even to interested persons like you and me. Our turn will come later."

"I don't quite – "

"We shall not get rid of each other very easily or very soon. That is impossible. Suppose an arrest is made. We shall be before the courts for weeks, and, at intervals, months, before the end is reached."

She smiled, and gave him a sidelong look which in any young woman who was not on the staff of a college of technology might be deemed provocative. He did not see it, however.

"That may be all very well for you," she said, "but what about my work? . . . Oh, my hat!"

Thinking the worst was over, she had released Tags in the doorway of the White Horse. He was tackled instantly by a stocky Yorkshire terrier—not of the toy species evolved for boudoirs and the Kennel Club Show, but a born fighter and quick on his feet.

The resultant uproar produced a crowd of loafers, not one of whom dreamed of interfering. Mannering, however, caught both dogs by the scruff of the neck and held them at arm's length.

"Here is your warrior," he said to Betty. "Who owns this one?"

"He belongs te t'hoose, maister," volunteered a voice.

"Then let him stop in the hoose!" And the tyke was dropped through a bar window into the lap of a young lady who was reading, as she imagined, all about the murder in the lonely farm.

She was annoyed, and said so, but Dunkeld appeared, and the rising storm was stilled as though by magic.

"Come this way," said the superintendent, indicating a staircase. "My fault, Miss Hardacre. I ought to have warned you that Foxton is notorious for its dog-fights. They provide the only excitement staged here in a blue moon."

Betty's colour was high and her eyes sparkling when she entered a well-lighted room and faced two men who were looking down into the street through a bay window which commanded a lengthwise view. They turned as the door opened, but, with the intuition of her sex, she knew that they had been watching her and Mannering approaching the inn.

Dunkeld's introduction was precise in its formality.

Chief Superintendent Winter and Detective Inspector Furneaux, of the Criminal Investigation Department, New Scotland Yard," he said, indicating a very big man and an almost remarkably small one. "Miss Hardacre, from the; West Yorkshire College of Technology, and; Captain Robert Mannering "—he paused a moment—"of the Indian Army, I think."

"Attached, until June, but now retired, with permission to retain my rank and uniform," said Mannering with the solemnity of a D.A.A.G. addressing a court-martial.

"We know all about both of you," said the big man genially, "but that statement is not so ominous as it sounds. Scotland Yard's principal occupation is the safeguarding of good citizens from the attacks of bad ones."

"Not one of my excellent Chief's best efforts," cackled the little man. "Allow me to explain, Miss Hardacre, that, in deference to your visit, he is not half smoking and half eating a fat Havana cigar. Being a creature of habit, he misses it."

"I'm so glad," sighed Betty. "I was just wondering if I might have a cigarette. My dog started a fight downstairs. He wasn't to blame, really. An undersized whelp sprang at him like a tiger, and I was quite upset until Mr. Mannering separated them."

"Thank you!" laughed Winter, who seemed to be much amused by her words. "I'm afraid," he went on, "there's not a cigarette in our pockets. Mr. Mannering and the superintendent are pipe-smokers, while I, as you have been told, affect full-flavoured cigars."

"You are aware, of course, of a pointed omission in that list?" said Furneaux.

"I take it that you are a non-smoker," giggled Betty, who, for one frenzied second, wanted to imitate Mrs. Lysaght.

"Exactly. I hope, too, you followed the really skilful way in which I also was indicated as 'an undersized whelp'? Isn't it marvellous how the mere thought of chewing a roll of poisonous tobacco leaf can brighten a heavy wit?"

The girl was utterly at a loss how to take these two. Surely they could not be on the verge of a quarrel!

"I hadn't thought of that until you pointed it out," she said. "What I do want is a match. I have plenty of cigarettes. And I am just a bit curious to know how Mr. Winter guessed that Mr. Mannering prefers a pipe."

"Are you puzzled, too?" inquired Winter, looking at Mannering.

"Oh no. I saw the three of you giving us the 'once-over' as we walked down the street, and you probably noticed that I put my pipe in my pocket," came the calm reply.

"And now that you have all taken each other's measure so thoroughly," said Dunkeld, speaking in a businesslike way curiously at variance with the humour twinkling in his eyes, "let us get to work. I wish the doctor could be here, but I cannot wait, as there are heaps of things to be attended to before I start you off for Blackdown Farm at ten. Do you two gentlemen wish to make any notes? Shall we need a table, I mean?"

"I trust to my memory, while Furneaux relies entirely on his imagination," said the Chief.

"Well—who begins?"

"Mr. Mannering."

Betty, who thought she knew all that her fellow-witness could tell, tried at first to form some sort of estimate of the Londoners. She was quite sure she liked them, but neither conformed in any particular with her preconceived ideas as to what manner of person a Scotland Yard detective really was. Mr. Winter's type was plentiful enough in Yorkshire, but his "doubles" were no hunters of men but of foxes. Had she been told that he was squire of many acres, a J.P., a judge at agricultural shows, he would have fitted admirably into the mental picture thereby evolved. Never could she have placed him as a high official of the C.I.D.

As for Mr. Furneaux, the description was lmost ludicrous. He was so small, so natty, dressed with such Savile Row accuracy, that he might have been a "star" actor in musical comedy—one of those mercurial little fellows who dance on nimble toes and can make an audience rock with laughter by merely saying "Tut-tut!"

True, there was power in each face. The Chief's large round head, prominent blue eyes, and firm chin bespoke strength of character and an indomitable will, whereas Furneaux's expression was one of sardonic intellectuality. She had noticed already that his sallow skin, matching black hair and eyes extraordinarily brilliant, was almost Japanese in its trick of wrinkling all over when he smiled.

But neither man was smiling now. Each was listening intently, and Betty soon grew aware that Mannering had gone through many exciting experiences which he left untold when he persuaded the Elmdale policeman and herself that a ghastly crime had been committed in the isolated farmhouse on the high moors. This was something altogether different, a story which cast a spell over its hearers, a reasoned analysis of an amazing adventure which passed swiftly from the commonplace to the realm of Greek tragedy. At first she was somewhat annoyed at finding she knew so little of what had actually happened. But that phase passed when she realised that he was speaking to a very different audience—a gathering of experts in which, by some miracle of chance, she was included.

When he reached the end she was positively startled by the first question put by Furneaux.

"Have you formed any theory," said the little man, "as to why Sir William Sandling was living in such seclusion in an outlandish spot like the edge of a bog?"

"Yes," came the instant response.

"What is it?"

"Sir William went there to study the genesis and action of marsh gas."

"That does not take one very far as an explanation."

"It would take a great many people out of existence if he had succeeded."

"Ah!" broke in the Chief. "You think that, do you?"

"I know it."

"But—actual knowledge! A serious claim! In the conditions, almost a dangerous one!"

A step sounded on the stairs, and Tags growled softly. He, in his doggy way, felt that the folk up above there might not want to be disturbed.

"Here comes Dr. Lysaght," said Mannering lightly, as though glad to leave the centre of the stage. "Ask him to repeat the story I told him last night, and you will understand."

CHAPTER 5: MANNERING IS ENLISTED

LYSAGHT admitted afterwards that when he entered the room he felt a certain tension in the atmosphere, as though there had been a hitch somewhere. Even the superintendent's introduction of the men from the "Yard" was curt and flurried.

Nor was Mannering's greeting altogether reassuring.

"Glad you've come, doctor," he said. "These gentlemen are tired of hearing my voice. Do you mind carrying on?"

"I?" was the puzzled reply. "What am I to talk about? Sir William's injuries?"

"We've agreed to stick to 'Mr. Hope.' But your professional verdict can be given later. I want you to tell them about the things we discussed last night—marsh gas, you know, and the incident which drew a rather disturbing comment from 'Mr. Hope' twelve years ago at Oxford."

"Why have you decided so suddenly that Dr. Lysaght's recollection of something you told him may be more valuable than your own first-hand evidence?" broke in Winter.

"I'm glad you put it that way," smiled Mannering. "I think you have guessed the explanation already. You three, representing the police, know, in all probability, the nature and importance of the experiments being made at Blackdown Farm. But the doctor does not hide the fact that he guessed accurately a week ago what was going on, while I, a mere passer-by, so to speak, drawn by the idle chance of a summer storm into close connection with a tragedy, can say now definitely that a gas of tremendous power was on the very lip of discovery if it has not been actually set down in a precise formula. If that is so, and you accept Dr. Lysaght's version of our last night's talk, you will be convinced that much is known beyond the limits of this room. It follows that 'Mr. Hope' was killed by people eager and determined to find out what he had done—not what he was I doing—they were well informed on that point already."

Furneaux nodded, as though Mannering's abstruse argument were a simple proposition in mathematics. Betty did not understand at all, while Lysaght and Dunkeld seemed to be turning the words over in their minds to extract a hidden meaning.

The Chief's attitude bespoke, at any rate, a readiness to let this quiet-voiced, resolute man have his own way.

I take it," he said, "that, realising the urgency of our task, you want to save time? Very well. . . . Dr. Lysaght, if you don't feel we are rushing you a bit, will you be good enough to comply with Mr. Mannering's request?"

"Certainly," agreed Lysaght. "As I haven't the remotest notion as to what was on the tapis when I came in, my not very important testimony will have the merit of being unbiassed, at any rate."

So, without more ado, he gave an almost verbatim account of the overnight discussion. Oddly enough, however, he seemed to be more impressed now than he was then by the significant fact that marsh gas could gather on a moorland road in such volume and density that it might be set alight, while no man of a scientific turn of mind could fail to be impressed by the far-seeing vision of a great chemist who discovered in the incident the germ of a new and destructive force.

"By Jove!" he exclaimed with genuine sur prise, "there's method in your madness, Mannering. If the appetite comes in eating, conviction may come by repetition. The more I think of this affair the more extraordinary it appears. Chlorine and mustard gases were bad enough in action, but I remember that a new gas, never used, was manufactured in bulk in America from a formula supplied by experimenters in University College, Oxford. It was terrific stuff, not an explosive, but

more akin to fire-damp in its action. I have often thought
– "

He hesitated.

"What's the good of imagining vain things?" he went
on, seemingly vexed at his own flight of fancy.

"I suppose you formed the opinion held by a great
many other men," commented Mannering; "that the war
collapsed when it did because the Germans realised what
was coming to them? Every bomb containing that gas
dropped in any given area would have destroyed all life
within a radius of half a mile. All life, mind you. Every
blade of grass, every insect, let alone human beings and
animals. As a matter of historical fact, the Armistice
saved Berlin by exactly three days. Of course, that is no
State secret. To-day every young chemist can supply the
formula. The Germans went one better about 1920, and
blew up a whole town while concocting some devilish
brew. My old friend, 'Mr. Hope,' would not blunder like
that, so he went to Blackdown Farm, and was bludgeoned
to death there yesterday by those who meant to discover
just how far he had succeeded in perfecting the latest
terror."

"What is methane?" put in Furneaux sharply. As no
one else answered, Betty. found her tongue.

"The chief constituent of marsh gas," she said.

"Good for you, Miss Hardacre!" chuckled Furneaux.
"Tell us more."

The girl blushed at finding herself the centre of
interest so unexpectedly.

"I'm afraid I wouldn't have remembered if Dr. Lysaght
had not spoken of fire-damp in mines, and we have to do
with coal in South Yorkshire, you know. Methane figures
in volcanic gases and in the decomposition of vegetable
matter under the surface of water, as in marshy districts.
It is associated with petroleum and can be distilled from
coal, thus forming about one-third of ordinary household
gas. About half as heavy as air, it becomes a highly
inflammable mixture when mixed with air or oxygen. I

could mention many more of its peculiar qualities, but you don't want a classroom lecture, I'm sure."

She paused, and laughed with some slight constraint.

"All this is mere textbook stuff," she went on, with charming candour. "It's part of my job, you know, to reel off screeds of that sort. Of course, it has to be accurate, but it calls for no great mental equipment. When one leaves the known for the unknown in chemistry, as in every branch of science, one steps off into the void. There is neither sight, nor guidance, nor reliable foothold. If you reach firm ground somewhere ahead—well, you have done something worth while."

"We are greatly obliged to you," said Winter. "Just to get back to the business in hand, I want to ask you whether you have mentioned the locked diary or Miss Bingham's letter to any one?"

"No. I—I meant to say something about them to Mr. Mannering while we were walking here, but Tags interfered. May I explain what I mean?"

"Certainly."

Well, I believed that Mr. Mannering told me everything yesterday. I know now that he didn't; not that he kept back anything of real importance, but Oh, I find it hard to make matters clear. You see, I hated the idea that I was hiding things from him when he had been so outspoken with me – "

She reddened again, but the Chief took her seriously.

"You acted quite rightly," he said. "That does not imply any lack of confidence on our part where Mr. Mannering and Dr. Lysaght are concerned, a statement which I shall prove to both gentlemen in a moment. But Mr. Furneaux and Mr. Dunkeld agreed with me that the diary, which we opened and glanced through, did actually contain the formula of a methane compound as deadly as anything Mr. Mannering has imagined. None of us really understood what we read—a fact for which I, at any rate, am profoundly thankful—but we were so convinced of the vital effect on the peace of the world if the diary had fallen into the hands of a possible enemy that an inspector and constable are now on their way to the Home Office with it, and will deliver it to a high official in person this evening. It is locked again, and sealed, and is now reposing somewhat uncomfortably on the inspector's chest under his uniform jacket, while both men are well armed. I tell you this to show what we think of your find in that broken box. Moreover, happily for ourselves, we six are in the same relative position—we do not know the formula!"

Winter uttered the concluding words with such grave emphasis that civilisation itself might have been at stake in that small room of a small inn in a Yorkshire country town. Through the open window came the noises of the fair-ground—the unmusical clash of steam-driven organs, the voices of people in the street beneath, the raucous cries of men inviting the youth of Foxton to shy at coconuts or try various games of chance, the almost incessant snapping of miniature rifles in a row of shooting galleries. Such utterly commonplace sounds they all were, so absurdly incongruous with the appalling interpretation which this eminently sane and trustworthy representative of the British Government in one of its most important executive branches knew his hearers must attach to his reasoned opinion!

Furneaux, of course, relieved the tension.

"No wonder you arrived on the scene yesterday accompanied by thunder and lightning, Mr. Mannering!" he squeaked. His speech was almost invariably high-pitched and apt to break into a veritable falsetto when he was excited.

"Are you likening me to Jove or the devil?" inquired Mannering instantly.

Betty ventured to laugh, and hoped the others would not suspect her of weak nerves. It was a good sign, too, that the Chief relighted his cigar, which had been allowed to go out for the first time in history, as Furneaux did not fail to remind him.

Winter merely brushed the remark aside with a large hand.

"In your wanderings round the world have you ever come across or heard of a Professor Vorhinoff?" he asked Mannering.

"Vorhinoff? I remember the name. Isn't he a Russian Pole, the Johnny who proposes to destroy locusts by clouds of monoxide?"

"I don't know. Your suggestion may well be correct."

"Well, I'm pretty sure he's the lad. We in India take a lively interest in locusts, you see."

"Have you met him, or even seen his portrait in a newspaper?"

"No. About the portrait, of course, I cannot be positive, but I could hardly fail to have noticed it, owing to his proposed war on an insect which is a real scourge in the half-tropics."

The Chief produced a fat envelope from a pocket. He took out a cabinet photograph, and handed it to Mannering.

"That is the professor."

Mannering scrutinised the picture. Then he passed it to Betty, who sat next to him

"Sorry," he said, with a smile. "His face is new to me. He looks an intellectual sort of chap, and bears no shred of resemblance to either of the men I saw yesterday."

Evidently he had dispelled a nebulous theory. Furneaux chuckled, Dunkeld was obviously disappointed, and Winter seemed to suspect his cigar of not being properly packed, because he squeezed it between thumb and forefinger. Then he selected a letter from the same envelope.

This is a note from Miss Beatrice Bingham which Miss Hardacre found among the papers in the farm," he said. "I shall read it aloud." He did so, without haste or stress.

Not an important document in itself," he commented. "The main points are that she mentions Vorhinoff, and that her employer did not trust to her discretion. But it takes on a new aspect altogether when we are assured that Beatrice Bingham, as a name, is a distinctly far-fetched English variant of Bertha von Buren. That, by the way, is only what I may term a well-founded surmise. Her passport shows that she was born in Dresden, of English parents, and registered as a British subject. The Binghams did really exist, and had a daughter while resident in Dresden in 1901. Both father and mother are dead, and we have no available record of their offspring beyond the account given by this young woman. However, let that pass for the moment. I mention the fact to show how an easy-going man like 'Mr. Hope' could be wheedled into employing her. She was peculiarly useful, a skilled secretary, an excellent linguist, and trained in Switzerland in the office of an analytical chemist. We are bound to admit that Germany is thorough-going in all her undertakings. What better assistant could an English scientist secure if he scoured the whole country?"

"Yet he did find one," said Mannering, rising to knock the ashes out of his pipe in the fireplace.

No one paid the least heed to Betty's change of colour.

"Yes, too late—unfortunately. He was a difficult man to handle. He resented any sort of protective supervision, and insisted on doing things in his own way. Mr. Dunkeld can show you the angry protest he wrote when the Elmdlale policeman called twice at the farm. However, we in the 'Yard' did succeed in persuading him to conduct his researches into methane gas without seeking his secretary's help. I haven't the least doubt that when the facts are published my department will be assailed from all sides for not safeguarding such a valuable life. Yet, if people only knew the trouble we take and the dangers we run in shepherding eminent men and women from the bomb, the pistol, and the dagger, they would be astounded at our constant success rather than irritated by an occasional failure."

"Ah, yes!" murmured Furneaux pityingly. "Look at him! Worn to a shadow!"

Betty laughed outright at that, but the "shadow," weighing all of two hundred pounds, instead of being annoyed, turned the other cheek to the smiter.

"Sorry, Frog!" he said. "I was carried away by enthusiasm for the moment. Now, Mr. Dunkeld wants to be off. You have a suggestion to make, I believe?"

"First," cried Furneaux, in a voice that literally cracked with anger, "let me explain the origin of that offensive epithet, 'Frog.' I happen to be the only official in the Yard who can speak French."

He paused, hoping that Winter would dispute an outrageous statement, but the Chief only looked sympathetic.

"So," continued the little man, "because I treat the accent and grammar of the French language with the homage due to the most perfect vehicle for expressing thought in the spoken word yet evolved by the human race, I am scoffed at by those who use even their own mother tongue inaccurately. But, what matter? Are you married, Mr. Mannering?"

"No," came the ready answer, though Mannering's surprise was unquestionably not assumed, while Betty felt quite pleased that some one other than herself was being quizzed.

"Any family or personal ties which may pre vent you from giving whole-time service during the next fortnight, or even longer?"

"None whatever."

"Very well. Don't get hot under the collar; I had to clear the ground. We want you to leave Foxton by the noon train to-day and call on Miss Beatrice Bingham to-night at Sir William's flat in Welbeck Street. She does not live there, but, in the indefinite conditions obtaining just now, she remains at her post until ten or eleven each night. Tell her you have known Sir William for many years, that you met him in Yorkshire, and have more than a nodding acquaintance with methane. Puzzle her, interest her, and make yourself thoroughly agreeable. If you put your heart into the effort, you should lure her out to lunch or dinner to-morrow. Should you succeed in making an appointment, ring up 'Victoria 7000,' and leave a message for Mr. Sheldon, giving the hour and place. Best of all, call for the lady and carry her off in a taxi. By Friday you should be on a fairly confidential basis, because Beatrice will be most anxious to draw out every atom of information you possess. On that day, not before the evening, you can reveal a horrified belief that the 'Mr. Hope,' reported murdered in a Yorkshire moorland farm, is really Sir William Sandling. By that time Mr. Winter and I should be back in Town. Indeed, we may return much earlier. Let Mr. Sheldon know where you live—in a big hotel for preference. Phone him when you reach London, and write Mr. Winter full accounts of your adventures and possible discoveries, especially any deductions you may make from slight incidents. Address your letters to the Yard. If necessary, send them by special messenger, but don't go near our headquarters yourself. The Department, of course, pays all expenses. I cannot give you more specific instructions. You must depend on the hazards of the moment. There is nothing dishonourable in your mission. We are not asking you to act as an agent provocateur, but we do think you may have been sent by Providence to help in laying bare a diabolical plot against this country. . . . Now, what about it? Will you tackle a difficult and, as it may well be, dangerous job?"

Mannering had been filling his pipe while Furneaux was speaking. He struck a match, and was about to apply it to the tobacco when the diminutive detective shot that final question at him. He did not hesitate a second.

"Yes," he said.

"Good! We thought you would not fail us."

"But—as a matter of form—how about the inquest?"

"Mr. Dunkeld will take care of that. His first words will be: 'From information received.' Dr. Lysaght will do the rest, and the inquiry then stands adjourned for a fortnight."

"Should I pass under my own name?"

"It will be safer. You may meet friends while you and Miss Bingham are lunching at the Ritz or the Savoy. Your references to the past will be all the more natural. Take Vorhinoff, for instance. You may run across him, or discuss him. If so, spread yourself on flights of scorpions—or is it locusts?"

"Both, I think. Am I at liberty to disclose my own active connection with yesterday's events?"

"Not if you value your life," broke in the Chief. "That very consideration nearly stopped us from seeking your assistance. Even now I am more than a little doubtful. Could that fellow at the gate possibly recognise you again after seeing you at fully six hundred yards' distance?"

"No. I never lost sight of that very drawback. I kept my face averted, lowered my height by stooping over Miss Hardacre's car, and humped up my rucksack until I must have looked like a camel. Moreover, I was in my walking kit, and my shoes were hob-nailed."

"Then that will be all, I think. Have you enough ready money for an emergency, such as hiring a fast car, for instance, or paying for a canard de Rouen a la resse?"

"About fifty pounds in notes and a letter of credit for five hundred."

"Most convincing credentials! Well, we split up now. The best of luck, Mr. Mannering! You, Miss Hardacre, come with us, I believe? Mr. Dunkeld is sending a car almost immediately."

"Why not use mine?" said the girl. "It holds three comfortably—four at a pinch."

"The very thing. How soon can you call for us?"

"In ten minutes."

They all rose, and the local superintendent hurried away. Lysaght would have gone with Betty and Mannering but the Chief detained him.

"Just a word about the professional details you promised earlier, doctor," said Winter.

Betty collected Tags. She wanted no more fighting.

"What a curious combination those two make!" she said, when the open street made it impossible to be overheard. "At first I thought them eccentric, especially the little man, but there is method in their madness."

"Ah! I'm glad you caught on to that," said Mannering. "It so happens that I have heard of them before, through one of our men in the India Office. They are the most famous detectives of this generation. When working together, which is nearly always the case in any serious affair, their success has been phenomenal. Furneaux declares that the Chief sucks his brains, while Winter blandly assures the authorities that he may become a nervous wreck any day because of Furneaux' s disregard for departmental regulations and legal procedure. In reality, the commissioner of Police gives them a free hand. You see, he simply dares not say he approves of what they are doing."

"It is pleasant to know that I shall be with them to-day, and longer, may be. My only regret is that you have become detached from the party. You seemed to understand them so well."

"Have you forgotten my prophecy, then?"

"What prophecy?"

"That you and I are linked by fate. You are far from being rid of me yet."

"I don't want to be rid of you, as you put it. Why should I?"

"Why, indeed? But it is nice to hear you say that."

"Are you looking forward eagerly to this strange mission in London?" said Betty rather hurriedly.

"Yes, in a sense. It may have some real importance. Unfortunately I am ill equipped for it. I have no experience of your sex, Miss Hardacre. My life has been passed in outlandish places. I shall not know what to say to that blessed girl."

"Oh, she'll lead you on all right."

"I hope so. Otherwise my sole resource is to wring her neck until she confesses."

"Well, you soon tried that method with me."

"I won't attempt any excuse."

"Oh, but really—I didn't mean to be catty."

"Then, as I see Mrs. Lysaght in the offing, you won't think I am rushing my fences if I tell you that letters to the India Office will find me. How shall I reach you? We should have lots to write about, seeing that the C.I. D. seems to have admitted us to the Inner Circle."

"My college will serve for the time being. I'll try and send you a line this evening."

"How good of you! I have never before found a pal in a woman. It promises to be a pleasant partnership, with illimitable prospects. Ah, there you are, Mrs. Lysaght! Going shopping?"

The doctor's wife beamed on them.

"Just the two I wanted to meet! He-he!" she vowed. "Do you like chickens? Ha-ha!"

"Next to ortolans, I worship them," said Mannering. "But don't cater for me. I am leaving Foxton at once."

"Oh, you don't say! He-he! Deserting us so soon? Ha-ha! Aren't you vexed with him, Miss Hardacre? He-he!"

"Frightfully, but he cannot help himself. Well, good-bye, Mr. Mannering! I shall look forward to meeting you at the Assizes!"

And Betty raced the dog into the doctor's garage. Mannering, too, wrung his hostess's hand with fervour, and bade her a hurried farewell on the plea that he had to pack his few belongings.

"He-he! Oh, my! What's gone wrong, I wonder?" gasped the lady. "I must worm it out of Arthur! Ha-ha!"

CHAPTER 6: THE CURTAINED WINDOW

MANNERING departed from Furneaux's instructions, or advice, in one essential—he decided to stay at his club in Hanover Square. He was known there, and would meet other Anglo-Indians, thoroughly dependable fellows whose friendly co-operation he might well be glad of. It was not yet a full day since a casual adventure had brought him face to face with sudden and violent death, and it needed no rare intuition to guess that life in London might be fraught with equal danger. Winter's hint was, of course, meant to warn him. He was well aware that in paying court to Miss Beatrice Bingham he was playing with fire, which, if it touched him, could easily scorch him out of existence.

That aspect of the affair did not worry him at all. Peril had been his not always silent companion during four years in France and eight in India. He was inured to it. When he undertook a harmless tramp across the hills and dales of his favourite county he thought he was safe from the terror by night and the arrow that flieth by day. But he was mistaken. The Furies had found him again, and here he was, ready as ever to meet unknown hazards with a smile.

So, before leaving Foxton, he wrote brief notes to Winter and Betty, giving his London address. They had set out already for the moor, and he did not run into either the doctor or Mrs. Lysaght. Once in the train he compiled a record of his experiences of the previous day and had it ready for posting at York. Superintendent Dunkeld had probably forgotten to ask for it. But that was immaterial. A clear statement, with special attention to times and distances, could hardly fail to be useful if an arrest were made locally.

He reached London at 6.15 p.m., and drove straight to his club. There he retrieved his baggage, and the valet set out his evening dress clothes. He owned a thoroughly reliable automatic pistol, an old friend of days and nights in the jungle. Nevertheless, after weighing the pros and cons of the problem, he elected to leave it in a locked trunk. It was not a weapon easily concealed in a dinner jacket, and he certainly would not carry it in a pocket of a light overcoat from which he might be separated temporarily.

On entering the dining-room he found his one time C.O. in India, Colonel Westoby, scanning the menu. They dined together, and the older man, having ordered cocktails, commented on Mannering's bronzed appearance. "You look as though you had just come off a liner, after twenty-one days at sea," he said.

"You are out of the reckoning by a couple of months," said Mannering. "I left India in June, but I've been living very much in the open air on the Yorkshire moors during the past week—hence the sun-brown."

"On the Yorkshire moors! Hadn't you a pal who would keep you a few days longer, and let you have a pop at some birds on the Twelfth?"

"I didn't know a soul. I am a stranger in my own land. Yet, oddly enough, I did come across an old acquaintance whose very existence I had forgotten, I am ashamed to say."

"Who was that?"

"Sir William Sandling, of Oxford—the gas expert, you know."

Westoby put back on the table the dry Martini he was in the act of raising to his lips.

By Jove!" he said, looking around as though to make sure their talk was not being overheard, "that's odd—deuced odd. You met him, you say?"

"I expressed myself carelessly, Colonel. By the merest chance I found out where he had dug in."

"Well, keep the knowledge to yourself, my lad. There's a lot of people in London and else where who are keen on obtaining that information. They simply mustn't—that's all!"

"Professor Vorhinoff is one of them, for instance?"

This time the older man emptied his glass thoughtfully.

"What are you getting at?" he said. His air was most serious. Mannering's seemingly careless comment had struck home.

It had not been made idly in the first instance. Mannering had a vague recollection of having been told that Westoby, after leaving the army, was given a temporary job in the India Office. If that were so, some useful hints with reference to Vorhinoff and his plans for the extermination of locusts might be forthcoming, and the merest scraps of reliable fact in that connection would be invaluable when he met Miss Bingham.

"Nothing in particular," he replied, being apparently more interested at the moment in a sole Colbert than in any Russian. "I heard that Vorhinoff wanted to get hold of Sandling, and the links were obvious. They run this way: Locusts, Vorhinoff, monoxide spray—will it work?—ask someone who knows. The answer is 'Sandling.'"

"Who told you all this?"

Mannering looked frankly puzzled. He disliked these misleading tactics, but could not see how they were avoidable at the moment.

"There's no secret about it," he said. "Vorhinoff's theory has been discussed widely in India and Egypt."

"Yes, yes, admittedly. What surprised me was the bringing in of Sandling's name."

"Nothing remarkable in that, I assure you. About a fortnight ago Vorhinoff was anxious to communicate with Sir William, but failed, because the trail was cut at a York bank. I hope I'm not butting in on affairs of State?"

Westoby laughed. His unease seemed to have passed.

"It wouldn't be the first time, Mannering," he said dryly. "You don't imagine I am anxious to keep any secrets from you, I suppose? What bothered me was the extraordinary aptness of your conjunction of the two names. You will understand when I tell you that Vorhinoff turned up at the India Office yesterday, and grew most excited when he could not find out where Sandling had gone. Vorhinoff is a crank, you knows but he's all right otherwise—thoroughly sound politically, I mean. Poor devil, I'm sorry for him, as for every decent Russian outcasted from his own country. The truth that he worried us more than a little. He was convinced, he vowed, that Sandling's life was threatened. I have a notion that he got the wind up rather badly in the Under-Secretary's office. The telephone was busy at four o'clock and afterwards. To-day, too, there have been ructions between departmental chiefs. But please let all this in at one ear and out at the other. I wouldn't have said a word about it, even to you, if you hadn't tabled the one topic on which my lips are sealed."

"That's all right, Colonel," said Mannering. "In any case, I'd hate to put you off a good dinner. I'll tell you later what I have in mind."

Westoby looked him squarely in the eye.

"Out with it!" he said bluntly. "When did you leave Yorkshire?"

"Noon to-day."

"What part?"

"A moorland town called Foxton, in the North Riding."

"Ah! Is Sandling dead?"

"Really—suppose we eat? Candidly, I'm ravenous."

"So that's the position, eh? Was he murdered?"

"Yes."

Mannering's mind had been made up some minutes earlier. The Scotland Yard men had trusted him, but they were leaving a good deal to his own initiative, and there could be no error on his part in seeking the counsel of an astute senior officer with whom he had shared grave responsibilities in the Far East.

"Too bad!" muttered Westoby. "I feared as much. There will be a frightful row if the whole truth leaks out. How much do you know, I wonder? . . . Forgive me for putting it that way. Perhaps you have no idea of the tremendous issues really at stake?"

"I may have. I cannot be sure. Have you read in to-day's papers an account of the brutal murder of an elderly gentleman named 'Hope' in a remote farm on the Yorkshire moors?"

"Of course I have."

"Did you know that 'Hope' was Sandling?"

"Let me explain. I am on the political side of the India Office. Sandling's actual work lay with the War Department, though he was in direct communication with the Home Office. But we are all more or less mixed up in certain activities, so I do happen to know exactly why our leading analytical chemist had buried himself away up in the North."

"Very well. I think the next word rests with me. You and I are now going to finish our dinner in peace; then, if you are free for an hour, I'll take you to my room for fifteen minutes or so, when we can smoke and talk without interruption. After that I shall leave you, though I want you to stand fast here until I return. I have a queer story to tell, and I need your help. How about it?"

Westoby beckoned the head waiter.

"Can you possibly hurry up that casserole?" he said. "Captain Mannering and I are rather pressed for time."

About half-past eight Mannering crossed Oxford Street en route to Welbeck Street. It was still light enough, thanks to the sun's adherence to a fixed time-table, no matter what alterations the legislature may decree for the clock, but a cold wind rendered an overcoat quite agreeable. He stepped out briskly. He was aware of an unaccountable feeling that the sooner he was back in his club the pleasanter would life be—insofar as that evening went, at any rate. The notion came unbidden that the ultra-respectable streets lying north of Cavendish Square were associated with human distress much more intimately than any other section of London. Nearly every bright and cleanly and comfortable-looking house was a doctor's residence or a nursing home. Thither daily in hundreds, if not in thousands, came suffering people seeking relief from every sort of ailment. Invariably they had to endure even worse torment if the surgeon's knife were the only remedy. Often they went to their death. He remembered his father going that way for the last time. A sad locality, for all its comeliness—the Mecca of sorrow and disease.

At the corner of Welbeck Street he knocked out the ashes from his pipe. Smiling grimly at the fantastic and morbid conceit which had gripped him so suddenly, he examined the numbers on the houses, and elected to walk up the opposite side of the street to that which held Sir William Sandling's residence. Nearing it, he saw that the place was in darkness. Not even in the semi-basement domestic story was there a light.

Instantly he yielded to a sense of disappointment. It would be too bad if he had taken a long journey and keyed himself up to an undertaking fraught with difficulty and possible risk only to find that his quest ended at the blank negation of a locked door.

Nevertheless, the external indications were favourable. The broad front steps were spotless and the brasses of knocker, letter-box, and latch-lock gleamed encouragingly. They, at least, had been tended since the storms of yesterday. Pressing an electric bell and knocking at the same time, in response to an engraved request that both should be done if an answer were required, he had not long to wait before a light appeared in the vasistas above the door. From the angle of the shadows it cast, he judged that an electric lamp had been switched on at a landing on the first floor. Soon its rays were merged in a stronger light coming from the hall itself, and the door opened a few inches, being held by a chain attached to a sliding bolt.

A young and pretty woman, hatless, but wearing a fawn-coloured coat and skirt, looked at him inquiringly.

Is Sir William Sandling at home?" he inquired, raising his hat with a smile of polite deference.

"No," she said.

"Ah! Too bad. I had every hope that he might have returned from Yorkshire by this time. Are you Miss Bingham, may I ask?"

"Yes."

She was hesitant, even suspicious, but the unexpected question brought a flicker of surprise into her somewhat prominent eyes.

"Well, then, if you will pardon this late call—I reached London from the North little more than two hours ago—I would like to explain why I am here. My business is urgent, in a sense, and you, as Sir William's secretary, may be able to deal with it."

"What iss your nem, plees? That is, I mean, have you a card?"

Mannering knew at once that Miss Beatrice Bingham was so nervous that she had almost reverted to type. Probably she had not blundered so badly during many a long year, because the English accent and wording of her second sentence were faultless.

"Certainly," he said, producing a pocket book. "I have mislaid my card-case, but I know I have some paste-boards here. You see, I have been travelling quite a lot recently, and one's belongings get shoved away and forgotten in all manner of corners.

Meanwhile, he sedulously avoided even the semblance of staring at the lady, having decided instantly that he must not attempt to be ingratiating or she would straightway close the door in his face. So he sought for and examined a card before handing it over.

"That's my correct description," he said, grinning amiably. "It would be too silly for words if I gave you some other fellow's card, wouldn't it?"

Miss Bingham read: "Captain Robert Mannering, Indian Army, The Bengal Club, Calcutta."

"Of course," he went on, in the same chatty tone, "I have a London address, too—my club in Hanover Square, where I am staying. I'll write that, and the phone number, if – "

The lady apparently made up her mind to unbend slightly.

"Let me undo this chain," she broke in.

When Mannering was in the hall and the door was closed behind him, she explained that, as she was working late, she had allowed all the servants to go to a theatre.

"And in London one has to be so careful," she added. "Not that I am afraid of burglars or sneak thieves, because Sir William's only valuables are pictures and furniture, but, when alone, I do like to have the option of refusing admission to people who have no claim on my time. Will you come this way? My den is on the first floor at the back. One is not disturbed there by motor-horns and other street noises. . . . This is my room. Will you sit there? It's quite a comfortable chair, so I avoid it if there is work to be done, though I'm bound to admit I was only killing time when you rang. Do you like Russian cigarettes? Perhaps you don't know this brand. I smoke nothing else, yet it is difficult to get them nowadays, with Russian trade almost at a standstill."

Luckily, he was not at a loss to account for Miss Bingham's rather dramatic change from curt frostiness to chatty geniality. She was too friendly, too obviously at ease. Moreover, the chair to which she motioned him had not been vacated more than a minute; its morocco leather was still warm, and there was a distinct impress of a large hand on the padded left arm.

When he sat down his back was to a heavily curtained window, and he was certain that the third person in the room for whose benefit the lady's remarks were intended fully as much as for himself was now standing behind the curtain. A sudden attack from that direction would be irresistible, so Mannering made the best of things by ignoring completely a danger which might be only imaginary.

"I haven't acquired the cigarette habit," he said, glancing casually at the fireplace and a big square table littered with that day's newspapers. "I'm a pipe fiend. Long ago I came to the conclusion that cigarette smoke is bad for the eyes, and therefore interferes with one's shooting."

"Oh, please fill your pipe if you prefer it."

"Well, if I may, for the few minutes of my trespass. You see, I came here to-night hoping I might meet Sir William."

"When did you leave him in Yorkshire?"

Mannering smiled. He was busy with his tobacco pouch, and was evidently unaware that Miss Bingham's voice had grown unsympathetic again.

"I'm afraid my reference to Yorkshire has misled you," he said, knowing that his companion had seized what she regarded as a favourable opportunity to glance at the curtain. "The last time I exchanged a word with my old friend was twelve years ago at Oxford."

"What is that? Twelve years ago?"

"Yes. Just before the war broke out."

"But, Captain "—she consulted the card, and almost spat out the name—" Captain Mannering, you told me your business was urgent."

"So it is. I am in close touch with the India Office, and I know why Sir William went to York shire. Indeed, I have reason to believe that he has practically finished the research work which took him there, and, as I, too, am interested in methane gas, I came here at the earliest opportunity to have a chat with him."

"Methane! Why should he visit Yorkshire to study that?"

"Just, what I want to know. While in India I had a good deal to do with tea-planting, which is one of the crops that suffer most horribly from locusts. There's a clever Russian, Professor Vorhinoff, who has some sort of scheme for dealing with the pests by a monoxide jet, but I'm pretty sure he would do more harm than good in that way. He'd kill locusts, of course, but the tea-plant, a most delicate growth, might suffer just as much from the cure as from the disease."

"But—I really know little about it—Sir William is not concerned with locusts."

"Exactly. I want to turn his thoughts that way. There is a lot of hot air in international politics just now, but I cannot bring myself to believe in any immediate demand for poison gas in warfare."

"That is a matter I don't feel qualified to discuss."

"Well, I'm awfully sorry to have raised such a serious topic at this time of night. My real intent was to try and make an appointment with Sir William for to-morrow or next day. Indeed, a friend whom I left at my club will be wondering why I am keeping him waiting so long. Will you be here in the morning? If so, may I ring you up and ask if you have any news of Sir William?"

Miss Bingham, whose peculiar mentality seemed to have passed through many phases since she opened the street door, was now fully mistress of herself. She had pushed away the papers on her side of the table, and sat with her left elbow resting on the edge. She held her cigarette in that hand, which also shaded her face.

"Yes," she said slowly. "I mean that I shall be on duty from ten o'clock. But I must confess I don't understand why you rushed here, so to speak, from Yorkshire, when you knew all the time that Sir William was up there."

Mannering laughed discreetly.

"I knew very little about it," he declared. "I wouldn't be here now if the man I met at the club hadn't told me that Vorhinoff caused a bit of a row at the India Office yesterday or to-day, and that no one could get in touch with Sandling. So I guessed he had come home quietly without informing anybody—just the sort of thing he would do. I guessed wrong—that's evident."

"Why didn't the India Office inquire here?"

"Ah, there you have me! If it comes to that, why do Government Departments always act differently from other people? . . . Well, my sincere apologies! I'll phone you in the morning, about eleven. . . . It's too bad you should have the trouble of coming downstairs again, but I suppose you won't feel happy if the chain isn't on the door."

He had risen, throwing his overcoat over his left arm. The woman stood up, too, but unwillingly, he thought. He was quite certain she was racking her brains for some pretext to detain him. Her eyes were narrowed somewhat. Though her slim figure was relaxed in a graceful pose, she was intensely alert. She reminded him of a lithe snake ready to strike. Yet her words were reassuring enough.

"Before you go," she said thoughtfully, "I think I ought to warn you that your visit has made me rather anxious."

"You don't say so. Why?"

"Sir William is no longer young. He is, perhaps, a trifle eccentric, but I have never before known him go away and conceal his address."

"Have you been with him long?"

"About six months."

Mannering smiled.

"Then I may claim to be better acquainted with his ways than you are," he said. "That is a regular trick of his. Once he scooted out of Oxford in the middle of term, and was next heard of in Persia, where he was investigating an oil-field. But I may be able to do something for you, too. This lad at the club probably has all the facts up his sleeve. I'll pump him a bit. It will be humorous if I'm privileged to give you the right story over the phone."

"To-night? I shall not go home till eleven, when the butler and the others come back."

"I'll try my best, but these officials are wary fellows, you know. It's no use trying to bluff them. I suppose the phone number is in the directory?"

"No. I'm glad you mentioned it."

He jotted down the number in his notebook. Not once did he allow his eyes to wander in the direction of the dark-blue velvet curtain, though he could have looked at it now quite casually. Indeed, he weighed the point for a couple of seconds, but decided against it. Above all things, he believed, he ought to avoid any show of special interest in his surroundings.

Miss Bingham followed him down the stairs. She had readjusted the chain when he came in, and appeared to fumble with it now, making more noise than was necessary, but not enough to hide from Mannering that someone had crept lightly yet swiftly along the passage on the first floor leading to the front of the house from the room they had just quitted.

"You haven't told me yet where you live in London," said Miss Bingham, with her finger on the latch.

"How stupid of me!" he cried. "Did you leave my card on the table? Well, here's another. This is my club."

He wrote, using the wall as a desk. Sir William's secretary was not satisfied with the working of the latch now. She tried it several times, saying the while that it needed oiling. At last Mannering found himself standing in the spacious entrance with the door closed behind him. The cool breeze, so chilly a few minutes ago, had become singularly mild and grateful. He halted a moment to put on his overcoat and relight his pipe. Then he strolled down the street in the direction of Cavendish Square, knowing full well that he was being watched from a partly raised first-story window. To make his observer's task easier, he crossed the roadway diagonally and stooped to stroke a black cat which purred at him from the pavement.

"You're a friendly little beggar, puss," he said. "Now, if I, like you, had nine lives, I wonder how many of them I've risked during the past thirty hours!"

As he neared Queen Anne Street, a man standing just clear of the line of houses in Welbeck Street said in a low but clear tone: "Captain Mannering?"

"Yes," was the astonished answer.

"I'm Sheldon! Turn up this way, and I'll walk with you to the club."

Two policemen, chatting at the next corner, separated and made off briskly, one heading west and the other north. The constable coming down Queen Anne Street paid no heed whatever to Mannering or his companion.

"I thought it best to have reinforcements handy," explained Sheldon in an even, matter-of-fact voice. "One never knows what these neurotic Slavs may be up to. Of course, they had no apparent reason for setting about you, and, if they meant mischief, we couldn't have saved you, but we would certainly have got them all right."

"Capital!" agreed Mannering. "If I had been shot or stabbed, they would have been hanged!"

"That's the size of it. Very seldom do the police have an affair arranged so simply. In fact, it was too easy. I thought so the moment Colonel Westoby rang up!"

"So I was the 'kill' provided for the tiger?"

"Not exactly that. We in the Yard are not quite so callous. But I knew that the fair Bertha was not alone, and would have warned you had you obeyed orders. Didn't Furneaux arrange that you were to get in touch with me before you went to Welbeck Street? Well, you reversed the procedure. Perhaps it was better so. You didn't know your danger. But, as the matter stands, if you were in my place, what would you have done?"

Mannering whistled softly.

"That's one way of looking at it," he said. "Of course, there are others!"

Chapter 7: A Four Footed Detective

BEFORE leaving Foxton with the C.I.D. men, Betty went to a local bank and deposited Sir William Sandling's money in her own name. The manager, who had evidently been coached by Superintendent Dunkeld, recommended her to draw a cheque for twenty pounds at once, and repay herself any out-of-pocket expenses she had incurred, as well as a week's salary.

"I shall see the agent who let the property to Mr. Hope," he promised, "and he will attend to the legal formalities with the dead man's solicitors. By the way, do you know who they are?"

Betty confessed that she did not.

"At any rate, that does not matter for to day," said her friendly adviser. "Mr. Dunkeld will probably get in touch with them. If you are in any doubt as to payments, come and see me. A good deal of money must be provided at once for the funeral, whether it takes place locally or elsewhere, but that detail, again, can be left over until to-morrow or next day. I understand that the near relatives are abroad, and they will probably cable their wishes. The body was brought here early this morning."

"Oh," cried Betty, "it is a real relief to hear it is not at the farm. I have said nothing, but I dreaded returning there."

"Well, there was every reason why the inquest should be held in Foxton, and not at a remote place like Blackdown. Are you a witness?"

"I—I think not. You see, I never met—my employer. He was—killed while I was on my way to take up the appointment."

"Ah, it is a sad affair, from every point of view. I understand you are being well cared for by Dr. and Mrs.

Lysaght. As I live over the bank, you need not trouble about business hours. Call at any time if I can be of the least assistance."

Which was kind and helpful. Here was a man who knew how to talk to a woman in difficulties.

The weather seemed to have settled into a fine spell after the thunderstorms. Betty was a careful but not nervous motorist, so the nine miles' run to the high moor was exhilarating. No stop was made at Elmdale, P.C. Paxton having remained at Blackdown overnight with a sergeant and another constable. The Chief occupied the dicky by virtue of his bulk. Furneaux and the terrier shared the front seat with the driver. Neither of the men seemed inclined for conversation, and Betty kept her mind on the winding road until Elmdale was passed. Then she did turn a questioning eye on Furneaux.

He winked at her brazenly. She thought she could do nothing better than wink, too.

"Excellent!" boomed Winter from behind. "The 'fly cop' of the Yard has met his match at last."

"Do you approve of that statement, Miss Hardacre?" said Furneaux anxiously.

"Is it a mere comparison or a form of proposal?" she asked.

"I place myself unreservedly in your hands."

"Oh, then I must ask Mr. Winter what he meant."

"Nothing really serious," said the Chief blandly. "I am merely guessing that Furneaux was looking for the first word from you, but, for once in his life, he has encountered a woman who can keep a still tongue."

"Was that really why you winked?" demanded Betty, smiling agreeably at the little detective.

"No. I was encouraging you—that's all."

"Dear me! What a mysterious remark!"

"It becomes almost lucid when I explain that the drooping of my right eyelid was a simple physical expression of a psychological impulse."

"My hat!" broke in Betty.

"I am not addressing your hat, but your subconscious urge. Don't you realise that when you came along this road yesterday at twenty-five per, you were running headlong into the year's most thrilling crime? Mr. Robert Mannering ran into it at top speed, too. Now, here you are again, pelting towards the unknown, and almost simultaneously he is racing in an express train in the opposite direction. If that isn't a circumstantial complex, I've never heard of one."

"Oh! Do psychologists talk that way?"

"No, but Furneaux does," laughed Winter.

"I pray you pay heed to what I say," went on Furneaux, with such a purposeful air that the girl could not decide whether to take him seriously or laugh at him. "My respected Chief has a great and well-merited repute in his profession, but he is not qualified by temperament or acquired knowledge to discuss the secret springs of thought. I am. You, of course, know—which he, alas I does not—that when a small non-magnetised wire is aligned near a larger wire heavily charged with electricity, some part of the current in the stout wire is transferred to the thin one. We call it induction, but we really don't understand why space is bridged in that way. If, however, two strips of metal can set up a hidden link of the sort, what may we not look for when two highly intelligent human beings like you and Captain Mannering come in close proximity with an epoch-making event such as the killing of Sir William Sandling? The majesty of the law, typified by our large friend in the dicky, says that such a thing is a mere coincidence. I, on the other hand, an undersized but quite efficient human induction coil, respond instantly to some subtle influence whose existence I am aware of, though I cannot say why or how. In effect, this means that while I keep in touch with you and your coefficient in Mannering, I shall look forward with confidence to the speedy capture of the ghouls who murdered Sir William. If, on the other hand, you are suddenly called back to your college of technology in Leeds, and Mannering to his jungle in Assam—well, Mr. Winter may succeed where I shall undoubtedly fail. '

Betty's first impulse was to describe his pseudo-science as nonsense, but she refrained. She was glad of it a moment later, because Furneaux went on: "For instance, this is the exact place where you first saw Mannering yesterday. You stopped your car about fifty yards ahead, just short of the dip in the road."

"Yes, but – "

"I may be making a fairly accurate guess based on Mannering's vivid description of the meeting. Yet he did not tell me that you had decided already to pull up and ask him about the farm, though the Elmdale policeman's description of the wood there on the left made it almost certain that the house lay behind the trees. Mannering has an air of distinction which might almost be enhanced by a tourist's costume. You felt rather lonely and out of the world on this desolate moor, and caught gladly at the chance of exchanging a word with a reputable-looking person of his type."

"You really are marvellous!" gasped Betty, whereat Winter guffawed loudly.

Furneaux shrugged his shoulders and extended his hands, with fingers spread and palms upward.

"The biggest—at any rate, the heaviest—brain in the C.I.D. will now propound," he said disdainfully.

"I'm fed to the teeth with that induction theory of yours," declared Winter. "It leads nowhere. It won't even ring a bell or turn on the light. And I'm really pained to think you would sink so low as to try and bamboozle a nice girl like Miss Hardacre by your cheap analysis of an action which might be expected from ninety-nine women out of a hundred."

"You hear?" hissed Furneaux. "He is attacking you now in his venom—classing you with the common horde! That is the true measure of his comprehension of the feminine nature—one per cent."

Betty laughed loudly, and, as might be expected, said quite the right thing.

"I don't profess to understand you two the least little bit," she cried, "yet I am quite sure I have great faith in you. Neither says what he really means, I imagine, but I should be very sorry for myself if I were an evildoer and you were on my track."

Which was an adroit assumption on her part, because those well versed in the strange methods of the "Big 'Un" and the "Little 'Un" of the "Yard" could have told her that they were most to be feared when bickering at each other like a pair of back-chat comedians.

Mrs. Birch was anxious to give Betty a faithful description of the removal of the body that morning, but the Chief promptly came to the rescue by asking that the work of classifying manuscripts and letters, begun the preceding day, should be completed now as speedily as possible.

"So far as I can judge at this moment, there is little to detain us here," he said, speaking in a low tone for the girl's benefit alone. "For all practical purposes, we might just as well be in the London-bound train with Mr. Mannering. Still, being on the spot, we have to examine the place thoroughly; moreover, we must confer with Superintendent Dunkeld after the inquest. Put on one side anything you think we ought to see at once. For the rest, a number of packing-cases were sent on this morning, and the constables will help in nailing and cording them. Kindly number each case with black paint, and keep a list of the contents. The acids and other chemical compounds in the temporary laboratory should be packed separately, of course. If you are sure they can be taken to London, all the better, but if there is any doubt in the matter, you may be able to stow them safely for transit to Foxton, where a government analyst will tackle them in a day or two."

"One word before you go," said Betty, halting at the foot of the stairs with the dog in her arms. "How about the documents in the front room?"

"Naturally, you will sift and arrange all papers, wherever they may be. Furneaux and I will be out of the house in a few minutes. The whole place will be at your disposal then. Anything else?"

"No. Perhaps I was really wondering about finger-prints."

"We shall find none. Those fellows never removed their gloves while in this house, you may be sure. Mr. Dunkeld made a hurried test yesterday of the clock and the china vase, which we must assume had been replaced by one of them on the mantelpiece. He only obtained smudges. I am still inclined to believe that the actual murder was impulsive, as Furneaux puts it, but Sir William's assailants were prepared to go to any lengths rather than fail."

"Please, Mr. Winter, do you think they did fail?"

"If they didn't, it may be a bad job for civilisation. If they did, we have Mr. Mannering to thank for it—him and his few burned matches."

Betty sped upstairs. Very soon, thanks to her earlier work, she had an assortment of bundles ready to be tied securely. Then, seeing the detectives and Paxton going toward the wood, she tackled the sitting-room beneath. She entered with trepidation, but was glad to find that beyond some damaged furniture and the broken window there was no evidence of the recent horror. It seemed so strange that she should be thus closely bound up with the fate of a man whom she had never seen, and never would see. There was an infinite pathos in the tragedy, too. She thought of the daughter in far-away Kenya Colony, of the son in India, and her eyes filled with tears.

By one o'clock she had completed her task. Sir William had brought to the farm only such accessories as were absolutely indispensable. He had made a few memoranda, mostly undecipherable notes intended as *aides memoires* for certain ascertained or possible compounds to be dealt with when he settled down to the written word. Obviously, the locked diary was the repository of his matured decisions, and that was now in safe hands and on its way to London.

When, helped by the policemen on duty in the building, some four boxes were packed and corded—the chemical appliances, with which Betty was thoroughly familiar, offered no real difficulty—she had a word with Mrs. Birch, who, of course, did not fail to suggest that the visitors would "mebbe like a bite to eat."

That meant finding the detectives. They were not far away. Furneaux was perched on a gatepost at the main exit, while Winter leaned on the gate itself, smoking. They knew of her approach long before she could hear what they were saying, which did not matter at all, though they promptly began discussing her.

"What are we to do with this girl?" said the Chief, blowing several small rings of smoke, through a preliminary hoop.

"Leave her in Foxton a day or two and then bring her to London," replied Furneaux.

"What for?"

"To assist the Home Office analyst."

"Do you mean with a view towards improving her position? I don't suppose her present job is a well-paid one."

"Anything may happen when she reaches town. There's Mannering, for instance."

"You rat! I half expected you to say that."

"Then why didn't you say it yourself, you fat lump?"

The last three words reached Betty's ears, as they were meant to do.

"You two quarrelling again?" she cried.

"It's the same old dispute—mind versus matter," chirped Furneaux.

"Well, I bring a message of peace. Mrs. Birch has roasted two plump chickens, with delicious curly bits of ham."

"But what are two chickens, howsoever plump, among so many?"

"Oh, these are for us. She says the police men had their midday meal at noon."

"So that is why Paxton left us an hour ago. Well, well. Why wasn't I born in Yorkshire rather than in Jersey? Then I might have been a fine figure of a man, like the Chief."

"It is a pity to keep those chickens waiting," said Winter, and even Furneaux seemed to agree.

"This moorland air would give an appetite to any healthy human being, irrespective of size," he cackled. "Moreover, the adjective 'curly,' as applied to fried ham, weds the commonplace to the sublime."

They did not dawdle over the meal. At its conclusion Betty gave Winter a small packet of papers.

"Look through those when you have a few minutes to spare," she said. "They contain names which may be of interest. One, Vorhinoff's, was mentioned in Miss Bingham's letter, but it occurs in another letter from a Government Department signed 'E.O.W.' in initials only."

"Can you pick it out at once?"

Certainly."

Winter glanced through a brief note. He handed it to Furneaux. The little man nodded.

"I wonder how many people really knew what was going on?" he said bitterly. "'When is a secret not a secret?' I'm not proposing a conumdrum, Miss Hardacre, but simply stating a bald fact, because the answer is: 'When it is revealed to a Secretary of State.' Every such highly placed official should be kept in abysmal ignorance of matters of vital importance to the national well being. Do you think the 'Yard' tells the Home Secretary what it knows? Not 'arf, as London puts it. And that is why he can dodge unpleasant questions in the House of Commons."

"Thank goodness the House will not sit for months," said Winter, announcing that they would depart for Foxton at three o'clock, and he would leave them to their own devices for an hour, as he had to write a long report to the Commissioner.

"Do you care for a little stroll on the moor?" inquired Furneaux.

"Just the very thing!" vowed Betty. When out of earshot of Mrs. Birch she added : "I hate this old house. I am sure a witch lived here about two centuries ago. How could that poor woman possibly go to sleep last night?"

"She is not gifted with imagination, I suppose. But she remains an excellent cook. Do you think that Marie Bashkirtseff or Mrs. Browning could have produced a meal like that with such primitive appliances? . . . This, I take it, is where the body was thrown into the bog while Mannering was looking?"

The change of topic was almost startling, but Betty pulled herself together.

"I believe so," she said. "It was actually found there," and she pointed to a patch of black ooze nearer the farm.

Furneaux swept bog and moor with a comprehensive glance.

"Now, you are a highly intelligent young woman," he said. "You have a mind trained in scientific precision. You heard Mannering's story yesterday. He made it live before our eyes. What, then, in your opinion, is its most marked gap, or lacuna, as you might say in your lecture-room?"

"The disappearance of the two men after committing the murder, and their return a few minutes later."

"Splendid! I wonder why Mannering did not comment on it."

"He seemed to avoid all theorising, and kept rigidly to that which he had literally seen."

"Exactly. The Winterian or deductive method. Now we shall try mine, the inductive."

He led Betty at a rapid pace around the northerly edge of the bog. A tiny stream appeared when the ground began to dip, but they were able to cross dry-shod by choosing rocks and firm tufts in the channel. Thenceforth they took a slanting course up the side of the hill, following a narrow sheep track. The rivulet fell more quickly than they climbed. Soon fifty yards of heather-clad slope intervened.

Tags enjoyed the outing immensely. He knew nothing about grouse, but could scent them. There were rabbits in the neighbourhood, too, and possibly a fox had wandered that way during the night. Betty, being country-bred, had been trained in the etiquette observed on land given over to sport. She would have called the dog to heel, but Furneaux checked her.

"Don't let him get too far ahead," he said, "but he won't do a ha'porth of harm, even if he does disturb a few birds. Though you and I are vastly superior to Tags in most things, when it comes to using our noses we are in the 'also ran' class."

So the terrier's enthusiasm was not curbed unduly. As it happened, there were no grouse on that part of the moor at the moment, nor were any rabbits visible in the ever-deepening valley, or "gill," as it is described in Yorkshire, which led steeply down to Duneham. The dense under growth was still wet after the heavy rain, and Betty's shoes and stockings soon became soaked. Though she uttered no complaint, she certainly wondered why they were taking this apparently aimless tramp, since it was absurd to assume that the detective contemplated any practical survey of a moor spreading for miles on all sides. Indeed, when they had gone some three hundred yards, and Furneaux halted, she was glad, having it in mind to borrow a pair of dry stockings from Mrs. Birch before leaving for Foxton.

But Furneaux was watching the dog, whose behaviour had changed suddenly from bounding excitement to marked caution. Instead of chasing ecstatically in any direction for no other reason than the sheer joy of life, Tags was sniffing, retreating, advancing again, but never crossing an invisible line which seemed to circle around a particular point on the nearer edge of the ravine.

The detective almost yelped with glee.

"What did I tell you?" he cried, his voice cracking in a falsetto. "Our four-footed ally has proved his worth. If you care to risk your skirt as well as your stockings, Miss Hardacre, come with me and you will see something, or my name is mud!"

Betty had said no word about her plight, but she was beginning to learn that this little man missed nothing. She plunged after him into the knee-high heather, and he motioned her to keep behind him, as though danger threatened. Beyond a somewhat pronounced and disagreeable smell, however, there was no bar to progress until they reached the top of a small but steep bank of earth. This had partly broken away owing to denudation by the stream, and it also formed a miniature rabbit-warren. Now it was simply littered with the dead bodies of rabbits, old and young, quite: a number of rats, and a stoat and a badger. Moreover, a long, shallow trench had been scooped in the yellow sand which lay beneath the broken roots of the heather.

"Grab your dog!" shrilled Furneaux. "While we are with him he might take a chance, though.... the majority of these poor victims of poison gas have been here since yesterday morning, and the danger-point is past."

"But what does it all mean?" gasped Betty when Tags was safe in her arms.

"I'll tell you. Then I want you to bring or send the Chief. If you come back with him, leave that most valuable hound tied up at the house. You have before your eyes Sir William's last test of the deadly brew he was evolving. He pumped some small quantity of the mixture into the burrows, and you see the result. The rats and the other robbers fell later victims. In all probability the men who killed him watched the experiment from some lair in the heather. When, not long afterwards, they were faced with the problem of disposing temporarily of his dead body they thought of this place, and began to dig a grave. Then came the thunderstorm, which may have hindered operations. At any rate, we know now why they left the farm and returned there, while the discovery of Mannering's visit during their absence startled them into adopting the much better plan of throwing their victim into the bog. . . .. It is remarkable how at every step their actions are marked by indecision, lack of foresight, carelessness, call their vagaries what you will. Their purpose was fixed—its means of realisation left to the chance of the moment. Hurry now, please!"

Betty needed no second bidding. In a few minutes she was pouring a breathless tale into Winter's ears. His placid smile was a tonic for frayed nerves.

"I knew Furneaux wanted to get rid of me," he said, pocketing the notebook in which he had been writing. "I think, though, we'll set all hands to work. We may be able to find out where those rascals hid, and there is always a chance that they may have dropped something—a match box, a cigarette case, a worn cuff-link—you never can tell."

The local policemen, Paxton especially, were far from gratified when they heard why they were wanted. But, as the Chief did not fail to point out, they were not to blame for having missed that which the dog had discovered. The flight of the murderers by another road, the burning of the clothes on a distant moor, even the retrieving of the body from the bog, had put a stop to any close search of the ground outside the immediate neighbourhood of the farm, while the lingering scent of the gas had driven away the carrion crows and other carnivorous birds whose quarrels and circlings would have attracted attention otherwise.

Paxton, too, was given a slice of the luck which he deserved, for he had worked really hard on this amazing case from the outset. The rain storms had obliterated any possible signs of a hiding-place in the heather. Even the many footprints in the rabbit-warren were mere shallow depressions in the sand.

Yet it was not good fortune alone which led him to a small hummock whence a distant view of the upper part of the gill was obtainable; having an objective in mind, he chose the right place. There he found a small key. Not even rusted, it could not have been lying out in the open longer than a day. Its shape was somewhat unusual, as it was flat and broad, and cut to fit a lock of at least four wards. Both Winter and Furneaux regarded it as by far the most valuable clue yet forthcoming. They left a more extended and prolonged examination of the surrounding moor to the men in uniform, and openly grudged Betty time to avail herself of the resources of Mrs. Birch's wardrobe in the matter of dry stockings before hustling her into the car.

But she stuck out valiantly for the few minutes' delay.

"If not I, at least my dog, has earned the right to save me from catching a violent cold," she protested.

"I grant Tags's claim," agreed Winter.

"I'm as wet as you," squeaked Furneaux, "but I couldn't wear Birch's socks if I tried."

"As a matter of plain fact," said the Chief, "you are not fitted to fill the boots, let alone the socks, of any other man here."

The very fatuity of the remark silenced even Furneaux, and Betty fled before he recovered from the shock. But she had been given one more demonstration of the occult way in which these two played into each other's hands. The executive head of the Criminal Investigation Department might reasonably have elected to devote a spare hour to the writing of a detailed memorandum for the benefit of an Olympian personage seated in an office at Scotland Yard, yet he knew full well that Furneaux would make good use of that same hour.

"I wonder what else they have learnt since they came here?" she asked herself. "Perhaps, if I behave, they may tell me!"

CHAPTER 8: SOME DISTURBING THEORIES

MANNERING was not long in discovering that Inspector Sheldon was as unlike the average detective of fact or fiction as either Winter or Furneaux. True, in physique he came closer to regulation pattern than either of those "extremes." He was fairly tall, well-proportioned, and thoroughly fitted to take care of himself when tackling a desperate criminal. But his quiet, unassuming manner, his air of philosophical detachment from the common things of life, his broad-minded views on matters concerning which he might be expected to speak with the official voice, became evident even during that short walk to the club.

For instance, he put a surprising question to Mannering before they were together a minute.

"What sort of man is Colonel Westoby?" he asked.

"Oh, a first-rate chap, shrewd, well-informed on a variety of unrelated subjects, and thoroughly dependable in a tight place," was the ready answer.

"So I should imagine. I have met scores of colonels and generals. They are all right when you know 'em, as the song says, but their stupid 'orderly room' airs are annoying at times. I believe in India you describe them as 'bahadurs' and 'burra sahibs.' I wonder if they are aware of it!"

Then Mannering laughed.

"Did Westoby seem to want you to click your heels and salute when you called at the club?" he asked.

"I—I rather think so."

"Well, forget it. He's one of the best."

"Oh, his Commanding Officer's parade tone didn't worry me in the least. Being a junior, I have to put up with it from lots of brass hats. But, if we're going to work with him in this affair you might contrive to give him the tip that the President of the Court-Martial, as such, counts for little with the 'Yard.' Of course, being a sensible fellow, he won't try any tricks with the Chief, but God help him if he regards Furneaux as a rather smart corporal and treats him on that basis."

"Great Scott!" thought Mannering, "what can have bitten Westoby?" for that most excellent officer and loyal friend did not seem to fit into the picture in any way.

Aloud, however, he said: "Something must have gone wrong, because Westoby and I were associated in India, and I always found him, if anything, rather diffident in backing his own opinion."

"I'm sure of it. My point is that he tried to give me orders, and was obviously peeved when I told him to sit tight till I returned. Do you appreciate the value of that word 'peeved'? It is quite the best adjective—and verb, too, I believe—that America has added to the language."

"He may even have been worried on my account," laughed Mannering.

"So was I. Well, perhaps the fault was partly mine. You see, we are up against a set of strange circumstances. When there are lunatics on both sides of the fence it is not surprising that some one should get hurt."

"Sir William Sandling was no lunatic."

"Wasn't he? He acted and seems to have thought like one."

"What on earth do you mean?"

"I don't know. One forms nebulous theories which are not to be set forth in precise language. Have you discussed this case fully with Colonel Westoby?"

"No. It was hardly possible. If he has any inside information coming through his department his lips are sealed, no matter how trust worthy he may deem me or any other man outside the official ring."

"Yes. Queer, isn't it? Heaps of people were aware of Sandling's search for a new and most potent gas. The Foreign, India, and Home Offices knew of it, in addition to the War Office—the one mainly concerned. Doesn't that strike you as odd?"

"That point had not occurred to me earlier,"

"More than that, the German Secret Service thinks it worth while to put their most skilful female agent on his track, and the Russians, White and Red, are crazy to get hold of his invention as soon as it is perfected. Some of these pests believe that that time is now, and Sandling has been battered to death as a logical result. Of course, you have not yet heard to-day's developments in Yorkshire?"

"No. Any arrest?"

"Nothing dramatic of that kind. The arrests, if any, will be made far enough away from Blackdown Farm. Furneaux was on the phone just before Colonel Westoby rang up. There cannot be the least doubt that Sir William made things easy for his murderers. He practically ordered the Birches to spend the day in Foxton. In any case, there was no need for husband and wife to be out of the house at the same time, but he insisted on it. Then he got Birch to send a telegram to Bertha, otherwise Beatrice, at three o'clock in the afternoon—he himself being then dead, according to your direct evidence—to the effect that she was to tell Vorhinoff he must wait ('decision will be made to-day,' was one remarkable phrase used). By Jove! it was justified, and no mistake. But what did it mean? Surely that he expected a visit from the very men who killed him, since it could hardly have applied to his experiments. Again, how could they have laid their own plans so thoroughly if they were not sure the coast would be clear? Finally, there's the test on the rabbits."

"Rabbits!"

"Of course, that came out after you left. The truth is that I have not yet digested this case thoroughly. Four badly rattled Secretaries of State have kept me on the jump all day. And in August, mind you, when London is empty! Take it from me, though, London wouldn't be empty long if the people whose absence gives rise to the saying knew what was going on. Do you remember August 4, 1914? That amazing date interfered considerably with grouse-shooting, didn't it? And Sir William Sandling was killed on the fifth. Odd, eh? But, maybe, I'm talking too much. I may say frankly I would have switched you on to the remarkable revival of dog-racing or the craze for Atlantic flights if both the Chief and Furneaux had not made me understand that you were well posted in this affair."

"I ought to be. I'm afraid I started it."

"What does that mean exactly?"

"I put Sir William on the track of marsh gas twelve years ago. But that bit of ancient history will keep. What about those rabbits?"

"Miss Hardacre's dog found them. She and Furneaux were walking over the moor when the fox-terrier led them to the place where Sir William tried his gas in the open on Tuesday, some time after ten o'clock in the morning, at which hour the Birches drove off to Foxton. Then, a peculiar key picked up on the moor showed that the experiment had been watched by others, almost certainly without the inventor's knowledge. Oh, it's a peach of a case—this Sandling mystery! Talking of peaches, Furneaux says Miss Hardacre is one, and he's no mean judge."

"If to be a 'peach' implies that she is a very attractive and intelligent girl, he is right."

Mannering's voice hardened, not unconsciously, whereat Sheldon probably smiled.

"Oh, don't you care for Americanisms?" was his disarming retort. "I like them. They are short-cuts to understanding. For instance, Furneaux put in one word what you expressed in—let me see—five."

By this time they were at the club. They had covered no great distance, yet Mannering had not only modified some of his views on the tragedy itself, but was also beginning to appreciate certain unexpected qualities in the personnel of the headquarters staff at Scotland Yard.

Westoby was the next to be disillusioned. He almost barked his relief at seeing Mannering.

"You're well beyond your time-limit," he growled, and his former colleague grinned broadly at experiencing what Sheldon termed the "orderly-room" tone.

"Couldn't help it, old thing," said Mannering. "I was detained by a lady. She was pretty enough, though far from charming. However, let's order drinks to be sent upstairs."

"The truth is, Colonel, you ought to lecture Captain Mannering severely," said Sheldon. "What is the first duty of a soldier?"

"Obedience," snapped Westoby. Such a question from a mere detective was almost impertinent.

"Exactly! He disobeyed orders. However, not for the first time in military history, he did all the better thereby. Now, do you mind telling me, apart from hearsay, no matter how well founded or credible, what you actually know about the present whereabouts—or fate, shall we put it?—of the gentleman in whom we are all so interested?"

Westoby was undoubtedly puzzled. But, rather wisely, he took his cue from Mannering's easy-going attitude.

"Very little," he said. "Indeed, nothing quite definite."

Sheldon smiled. The other men, as he was well aware, had just noticed a peculiarity in his eyes, the pupil of the right one being markedly larger than that of the left, and they were quite candidly staring at him.

"You hear, Captain Mannering?" he said. "Before we go to your room, ring up Miss Bingham as arranged, and tell her you have no news, but will phone her again in the morning. You have seen Colonel Westoby. He has told you nothing. That will be wholly true and thoroughly misleading."

Mannering got in touch with Sir William's secretary within a few seconds. Even as she answered the call he heard a chair being moved in another part of the room. Yielding to an impish impulse, he remained silent for a few seconds, and thus probably conveyed a momentary suspicion that he had been listening intently.

"I'm sorry," he said then, "but this wizened old Anglo-Indian friend of mine can add nothing to what we know already. At least, that is how he puts it. But I am certain to run across some fellow in the morning who'll be more inclined to talk. Tell you what—let me call for you about one o'clock to-morrow and take you out to lunch. Then we can discuss the affair at our leisure."

"Come to luncheon to-morrow? Oh, I'm afraid I can hardly do that!"

"Why not? One has to eat, though the heavens fall."

"But—what 'affair' have we to discuss?"

"The strange silence of Sir William Sandling, of course."

He was well aware that the lady was practically repeating his words for the benefit of some interested third party. Her reply was convincing. She had been bidden to accept.

"Well," she said, with coy hesitancy, "I mustn't be out of the house for more than an hour."

"Righto! We'll hop into a taxi sharp at one."

"Will you please choose some restaurant not too far away?"

"How about Claridge's, or the Ritz?"

"Aren't they—rather—fashionable?"

"Possibly, but the food is good, and I am not often honoured by a lady's company at meal-times."

"Then, shall we say the Ritz?"

"The Ritz it is. Au revoir sans adieux!"

He rejoined the others. They seemed to be getting along all right. Westoby was laughing at something Sheldon had said, so the ice was broken. Mannering retailed his brief conversation.

"Your amiable fraulein is clumsy," commented Sheldon. "We know now that some of her associates will be waiting in the foyer and follow you into the restaurant. We must try and do better than that."

"Will you be on hand, too?" inquired Westoby. "May I invite you to join me there about that time?"

"Sorry, sir," smiled the detective, "but none of this crowd must set eyes on me yet. There's no reason, however, why you and a friend should not lunch there. It may be quite useful that you should be able to recognise Miss Beatrice Bingham and other members of her gang at some later date. If some of them enter the restaurant, I'll take care to let you know where they are seated."

By this time the three were in Mannering's room, and Westoby produced a well-filled case of Burmese cheroots.

"Black but comely and well matured. You remember them, Mannering?" he said.

"Perfectly. When put to the test, they reveal the white ash of a blameless leaf."

Westoby shook his head.

"Don't sharpen your wits on me to-night," he muttered wearily. "I'm anxious, and have no desire to conceal the fact. I wonder if you two really know what sort of thunder-cloud is darkening the political sky at this moment?"

"I do, I think," said Sheldon.

"And I can make a fair guess," put In Mannering.

"I may be exaggerating the actual danger, but I am convinced that if Sir William Sandling has converted an amazing theory into its ultimate practical form, and the knowledge is communicated to certain evil-minded men, it will not be a question of one-half of the world not knowing how the other half lives, but of a phenomenally widespread ignorance of the way in which the other half has died."

"Bad as that, is it?" said Mannering.

"That is one way of looking at it," announced Sheldon gravely. "If one could only be sure that the bad half could be dealt with so thoroughly! But I must not say that, I suppose. Who am I that I should dare decide how humanity should be portioned out? But I can advance one thesis without fear of error. If Sir William Sandling's work was so important, why in the name of common sense was he allowed to do it under such absurd conditions?"

"Why was he allowed to do it at all?" said Mannering.

"If not he, it would be another," growled Westoby. "Goodness knows how sick I am of this plotting and planning to make men better by killing them! As a soldier I have seen too much of that monstrous method. Yet how was one to deal with Sandling? He is, or was, our greatest chemist. He was obsessed with some fantastic scheme which would convert marsh water into a deadly gas, capable of spreading over an area limited only by the extent of the marsh and the direction of the prevalent wind.

We could not imprison him, either in gaol or a lunatic asylum."

"That's twice to-night I have heard my old friend's sanity called in question," broke in Mannering.

"Twice?"

"Yes; once by you, and earlier by Sheldon—each time inferentially, of course. Have we, then, forgotten his services during the war?"

"I am forgetting nothing. I wish I were. I may not have many years to live, but I have no desire to be given a momentary glimpse of some miasmic vapour creeping in through every joint in door and window of this room, and fading out of existence forthwith. If the notion is hateful to me personally, it is equally hateful to think of it as applicable to my fellow human beings."

"Well, it won't happen just yet awhile," said the detective coolly. "I cannot speak positively, because there may have been a hitch somewhere, but my direct Chief, Mr. Winter, believes that Sir William's secret is now safeguarded in the Home Office, and, if it cannot be protected there, the sooner we are all good Bolsheviki, the more chance we have of escaping asphyxiation, though I imagine it is death by flame rather than poison we have to dread most. Isn't that how the world is to be destroyed next time? And now, gentlemen, I must be getting back to the Yard—and so to bed, I hope. . . . You'll not be stirring forth again to-night, Captain Mannering?"

"No. I don't feel a bit like it."

"Better so. Though I think you're safe enough until after you have lunched with Miss Bingham. Thenceforth, you must watch your step. Of course, it's a trite remark, but you won't be tempted to nod affably if you run into me unexpectedly to-morrow about 1 p.m.?"

"I shall have eyes for no one except the lady."

"I hope you really mean that. I know quite well that both you and Colonel Westoby are old hands at the espionage game, but the Indian frontier and London are very different places. Piccadilly can be dangerous as any jungle, even in broad daylight. Pardon this bit of advice. My excuse is that such things are better said needlessly than too late. If anyone rings up from the 'Yard' during the next ten minutes, will you tell the inquirer that I am hurrying there in a taxi?"

Westoby was manifestly ill at ease after the detective's departure.

"Smart chap that," he muttered. "Have you any notion what he meant by saying that Sandling' s discoveries are now known to the Home Office?"

"Oh, I think I can explain what he had in mind," and Mannering told of the locked diary found by Betty among the books in the savant's bedroom at the farm. He had not felt wholly justified in mentioning it earlier, and his senior was grimly amused now at the way in which they had fenced with each other.

"My position in this affair is one of singular difficulty," growled Westoby. "Actually, I am supposed to know nothing beyond Professor Vorhinoff's plan for exterminating locusts. But that, of course, is mere eye-wash. Vorhinoff, a White Russian, wants to get rid of Bolshevism, and the more wholesale the method the

better he will like it. You remember the part the
Masurian Marshes played in the war? Hindenburg and
Ludendorf, and a lot of other Huns, are quarrelling now
as to whom the credit for Russia's defeat there was really
due, but, if poor Sandling's scientific dream comes true,
what the Germans did to the Russians then won't be a
patch on the damage his invention would inflict on them
now. There you have the whole wretched business in a
nutshell. You see where our Government stands? It would
be one thing for the British War Office to control a most
potent weapon if the future welfare of the world
demanded its use, but quite another that it should be
employed by irresponsible theorists like Vorhinoff."

"Or Sandling himself?"

"It may be so. I don't want to do him an injustice, even
in thought, but it does seem strange that he should refuse
the protection and wide scope for practical demonstration
which both the War Office and the Admiralty could have
given him in a dozen different localities. 'Pon my honour,
one is forced to admit that Moscow would have looked
after him more efficiently, though they might have shot
him the moment he had demonstrated that his scheme
was practicable."

The two talked until a late hour. They did not meet
next morning, because Mannering breakfasted in his
room. He was disappointed, and a little surprised, that
there should be no letter from Betty. She had promised so
definitely to write that he decided to ascertain whether
Dr. Lysaght's house was on the telephone. However, that
could wait a while, so he devoted a solid hour to scan the
columns of every morning newspaper he could lay hands
on. Moreover, a hint from a newsagent's shop sent a
messenger to the bookstall at King's Cross, where the
leading Yorkshire dailies were obtainable.

The local papers, of course, published fuller reports of
the inquest than could be looked for in London, but the
police chiefs had arranged matters so astutely that no
hint of Sandling's identity or purpose in life was allowed

to escape. To all outward appearances the murder of a practically unknown elderly man in a remote moorland farm was the work of some predatory wretches who were prepared to kill rather than miss the small booty they might secure in such circumstances.

In one instance, however, the writer of a leaderette in a Leeds paper came so perilously near the truth that Mannering wondered if some one in Betty's College had not guessed what had actually happened.

"This seemingly unpremeditated and senseless crime," wrote the journalist, "contains certain elements of mystery which call for thorough investigation. Who was Mr. William Hope? Why was he living a hermit-like existence in such an inaccessible place? It is not as though his habits and personality were known to his moorland neighbours. He had not dwelt in the district many weeks, and the farm itself had been derelict for years until, at his behest, an estate agent put the house in order and supplied the necessary furniture. Here are several well-defined lines of inquiry, and it may be taken for granted that the North Riding police will follow up each and every avenue until the facts are established. At present the commonplace explanation of robbery with violence culminating in the victim's death does not carry conviction."

The same newspaper gave the most detailed account of the inquest, so Mannering cut out both editorial comment and report, and put the slips in his pocket-book.

Then, the weather being fine, he went downstairs, got the operator to put in an inquiry for Lysaght, and, after that arranged itself one way or the other, he meant taking a stroll down Regent Street. In the hall-porter's office he found the expected letter from Betty. It had come in by the second morning delivery!

The contents were brief but wholly to the point. They ran: "DEAR MR. MANNERING,

"I have just heard that the London post leaves in twenty minutes, and I have barely time to fill one small sheet and dash to the post-office. Mr. Furneaux will telephone Mr. Sheldon this evening, so he bids me say that you are to ask Mr. S. for full particulars as to the poisoned rabbits and the key found on the moor. Tags, to his great glory, is responsible for the poor bunnies, and Paxton lighted on the key. I may say at once that those things came about so naturally that they might almost have been arranged beforehand by the Scotland Yard men. Of course, you won't misunderstand that remark. I can't even strike it out and try again. But W. and F. are such genuine oddities, aren't they? I have been wondering if this third detective, Sheldon, differs from them as greatly as they differ from one another. If so, I am longing to meet him, of which there is a slight chance, because Mr. Winter hints that the Home Office may offer me some temporary work in connection with this case.

"I suppose you cannot find time to write this evening, but please phone me to-morrow early. Dr. Lysaght's number is 'Foxton 20.' And do take care of yourself. I am beginning to dislike Miss Beatrice Bingham intensely. You will grasp the true inwardness of this otherwise unfair and seemingly unwarranted comment when I tell you that I have read several of her letters, and they ring false throughout. Try and avoid her. I am sure she is a dangerous acquaintance. Well, this must be my last word for the moment.

"Yours sincerely,

"ELISABETH ANN HARDACRE.

"P.S.—Now you know the worst. When my brothers wish to infuriate me they call me 'Lizar Ann.' If ever you begin a letter intended for me in that way I shall not fail to grasp your full intent."

Mannering was striving to fathom the significance of the postcript when he was called to the phone. After the usual preliminaries he heard a woman's voice.

"Is that Dr. Lysaght's house?" he asked.

"Yes. He-he! Mr. Mannering, isn't it? Ha-ha!"

"Oh, Mrs. Lysaght! You sound cheerful up there in the North. May I have a word with Miss Hardacre?"

"He-he! I've sent for her. When the operator said 'Long Distance,' I knew it must be you. Ha-ha! Here she comes now! He-he!"

The line was so clear that Mannering could distinguish the very handing over of the instrument.

"That you, Mr. Mannering?" came Betty's distinct and well-bred voice.

"Yes. How is everything this morning, Betty?"

"Well—er—"

"That's all right, I hope? I am only obeying instructions. If ever I want to quarrel I am to address you as Lizar-Ann. Surely the converse holds good, too?"

"Oh, don't be stupid! You've gone and driven out of my head everything I meant to say."

"Let me give you a lead. I called on your opposite number in London last night, and was quite thrilled, not so much by her many attractions as by the fact that some nasty fellow was hidden behind a curtain. I had to sit with my back to him, too."

"Oh, I knew it. I was sure – "

"Never mind. Let us exchange opinions by post. I am lunching with the lady at the Ritz, so I'll write later."

"Yes, I know. Mr.—the little man told me—about the luncheon, I mean. He also asked me to advise you that there is no longer any need for secrecy. Half a dozen skilled reporters are here, including two special correspondents from London. There is a leakage somewhere. To morrow, perhaps this evening, some of the facts, and certainly 'Mr. Hope's' identity, will be published far and wide."

"Ah! That means I am free to speak without reserve?"

"It may be so. I wish you were not mixed up in that part of the business. At any rate, those are his exact words."

"Righto. Tell him how I interpret them. I shall be in this club between noon and half-past in case he has any criticism to offer. You must have had a lively time yesterday after I left. My congratulations to Tags!"

"He is listening-in now. But you will be careful, won't you?"

"Certainly, if only to save you from any unnecessary anxiety. Of course, I run no possible risk in a smart restaurant. The only attack I need fear there may be made on my ready cash."-

"Three minutes!" broke in a voice.

"Good-bye, Betty!"

"Good-bye-ee, Bob!—three Bob really!"

Mannering halted in the entrance-hall to fill his pipe.

"Things are quiet in town just now, sir," said an affable hall-porter.

"I suppose they are, to an old Londoner like you," said Mannering. "Now I, fresh to life here, find the pace rather swift."

"I don't doubt it, sir. It all depends on the point of view. You're thirty an' I'm sixty, an' that's about the size of it."

The man's philosophy appealed to Mannering, who, in his stroll through Regent Street, found himself wishing that Betty Hardacre could have shared it—the stroll, not the philosophy. As a mild pastime there is nothing a man enjoys more than an hour's shop in the company of a pretty girl who is not his wife.

CHAPTER 9: CLOSE QUARTERS

MANNERING pressed the electric bell at the Welbeck Street house about five minutes to one.

He assumed—wrongly, as it happened—that Sir William's German-born secretary, be her parents English Binghams or Teutonic von Burens, would resemble every other woman of his acquaintance in lacking the virtue of punctuality.

He gave his name and errand to a worried-looking butler. It was odd to note how the man's face brightened perceptibly at once, and Mannering believed that the change was due to the fact that he was English—a somewhat surprising explanation considering the locality.

"Yes, sir. This way, if you please." And the butler showed him into a reception-room on the ground floor.

A minute later he came back.

"Miss Bingham will be with you almost immediately, sir," he said. Then, sinking his voice to a confidential whisper, he added: "Beg pardon, sir, but have you any news of Sir William?"

"Nothing definite."

Mannering hardly expected such a question, yet he had no doubt of its motive. Here was a trusted member of the household staff genuinely concerned as to the well-being of a respected employer.

"Well, sometimes no news is good news," sighed the butler. "Will you kindly not mention the fact that I made the inquiry, sir?"

"Certainly. If you like, call at my club at four o'clock, or seven, or nine, and we can have a chat."

"Yes, sir," came the smooth reply in the deferential tone of one who, standing by the half-open door, had to raise his voice a little to make himself heard. "I'll tell the driver he may have to wait a few minutes. . . . Oh, here is Miss Bingham now."

The lady tripped swiftly down the stairs. She was neatly and expensively dressed, and shod in the steel-grey tints of the hour. Her face might have been made up, but her cosmetics were not treacherous. Indeed, she was very good looking, and wore her clothes most becomingly.

"Well," she cried, with a cheery smile, "unless our clocks are all wrong, I'm actually ready before time, Captain Mannering."

"I am always prepared for miracles on a fine morning in London," he said.

"Where are we lunching—the Ritz, isn't it? . . . I don't suppose any message will come through during the next hour "—this to the butler—" but if I am wanted, Wilkins, you will know where to find me."

"Yes, miss. Do you wish me to give you a call?"

"Certainly, if it concerns Sir William. Any body else must wait."

The change of manner in addressing a servant was slight but perceptible to an ear on the alert for the faintest indications of this young woman's social upbringing. The veneer was English, but the ingrained habit of thought was Prussian.

Now, Mannering was utterly at a loss how to proceed with an undertaking in which there was so little guidance. Trusting to the chance of the moment was all very well in its way, but he elected to get on better terms with this sprightly secretary before they even reached the hotel. So he risked an immediate rebuff. No sooner were they seated in the taxi than he affected to lose his balance when the vehicle swung round from the kerb. Catching Miss Bingham's arm as though to steady himself, he half turned.

"I wish now I had suggested an earlier meeting and hired a private car," he said. "Then I might have taken you out of Town, if only as far as Richmond or Harrow."

She pressed his hand encouragingly with her upper arm. It would appear that Mannering's opening move was in order.

"That would have been nice," she purred. "Of course, I dared not have gone far, because of the uncertainty. I am horribly afraid that—but we don't want to look sad when we reach the hotel, do we? Let us not talk yet about the reason of our meeting."

"Perhaps we can manage a short run after luncheon? It should be easy enough to arrange for a car by two o'clock, and you can phone Wilkins, you know."

"Impossible—to-day. You are not leaving London very soon, I hope?"

"Not for a week, at least. I'll make it two if need be."

"And then, you join your—family somewhere?"

"I have no family. I am absolutely alone in the world. Of course, you hardly realise what it means to a man of my age to be out of England twelve years on end."

"No friends here—in this city, I mean?"

"Only some fellows I've served with, and even they, in August, must be scattered over the map, on the moors or at the seaside."

"Don't you take a lady out to lunch or the theatre occasionally?"

"Fortunately I'm taking one out now. The theatre, plus a dinner, will follow in due course."

She tapped his fingers in playful reproof.

"You know I didn't mean that," she sighed. "I was thinking of some other lady."

"The last lady I dined with and accompanied to a theatre afterwards in London was my aunt, early in 1914. She, poor soul, was killed during an air-raid in 1917."

"Are you quite serious?"

"I'm telling the truth, anyhow."

"But you have met another young lady recently—the girl who was to have supplanted me in Yorkshire? Is she nice?"

The mere form of the question gave Mannering half a second's warning of what was to come, else his grasp of a well-rounded   arm   might   have   advertised   the astonishment he undoubtedly felt. And he had to decide in an instant on the rig line. He took it boldly.

"Yes," he said; "that is, if you are alluding to a Miss Somebody or Other whom I ran into at a doctor's house in Foxton last Tuesday evening. She is quite smart in a professional way, which is only what one would expect from a lecturer on science or something of the sort."

"Don't you know her name?"

"I cannot quite recall it at the moment. If heard it I might recognise it."

"Harding?"

"By Jove! that may be it. At any there's a close resemblance. How did you to hear of her?"

"Oh, I am bound to acquire information affecting Sir William."

"Well, I cannot be sure the name is Harding. You see, we met at Dr. Lysaght's place at Foxton, and I was so interested in coming across a sort of clue to my old friend's whereabouts that I gave little heed to the lady herself."

"Had she been employed by Sir William for some time?"

"I really cannot say. Certainly I didn't ask her straight out, but my impression is that she was just about to join him, whereas he had gone off rather mysteriously."

"You met her for the first time on Tuesday?"

"Unquestionably."

"And you left Yorkshire early yesterday?"

"At eleven a.m. exactly."

"You did not see her again?"

"At breakfast. I got away from Foxton myself as quietly as an otter slipping into a stream."

"I don't quite understand."

"No one up there cared a pin about my comings and goings, and I had a sort of notion that Sir William might have returned to London. That is one reason why I rushed off, hoping to catch him here. He certainly was not at Foxton."

The taxi drew up at the Piccadilly entrance to the Ritz, and the fact seemed to disconcert Miss Bingham strangely.

"Why is the man stopping here?" she inquired, leaning forward to free her arm.

"I told him to take us to the restaurant."

"Do you mind if we go to the other door—the main one in the side street? I want to have a word with the telephone bureau in case Wilkins rings up."

Mannering was well aware that this self possessed young woman wished to be seen with him as they entered the hotel. Though her adroitness was admirable, he determined that she should not be allowed to have matters all her own way. A slight obstinacy on his part in this quite trivial matter might be helpful later.

"It will be a deuce of a job for our driver to make such an awkward turn in heavy traffic," he said. "We can reach the foyer from this door in half a minute."

She yielded gracefully enough. Once in the hotel, she made straight for the Arlington Street lobby, asked an employee to direct her to the telephone booth, led Mannering there, and gave her name to the chief operator.

"Now," she laughed, gazing up at her tall escort coquettishly, "I'm altogether at your service. Please forgive my nervousness. You see, I absolutely must be within call if needed."

He was specially careful not to stare at any of a dozen small groups of people standing or seated in that part of the hotel, but it was amusing to note that even Sheldon, tucked away unobtrusively in a corner with another man, was rather taken aback by the unexpected appearance of the two almost at his elbow.

Soon he was interviewing the maitre d'hotel, and had secured a pleasant table whence Miss Bingham could survey most of the lively crowd gathering for the first social event of the day. Out of the tail of his eye he discovered Westoby and another Army man already entrenched near a window.

An amicable little wrangle took place as to which seat Miss Bingham should occupy. She vowed that she preferred not to face the light, though Mannering was sure she wanted to keep an unobtrusive watch on all who entered or left the restaurant from the main body of the hotel. Of course, he fell in with her whim. It could not be helped that the change should bring him and not his companion in full view of Westoby and his friend.

Cocktails were served. The lady protested she never touched spirits of any kind.

"At least, I mean nearly neat alcohol," she explained. "Please may I have something to drink that I really like?"

"That is exactly why we are here," smiled Mannering.

"Well, it's not bad form any longer to speak of German wines. Will you order a nice hock?"

"I admire your taste. If the world were even partly civilised, the Champagne district of France and the slopes of the Rhine would have been placed out of bounds during the war."

"That's twice you have mentioned the war," she said. "I never give a thought to it. I was only a small child when it broke out, and was promptly sent to Switzerland to be away from it all."

"You were lucky to be able to make the journey."

The comment seemed to puzzle her for an instant.

"Oh, of course, you don't know I was born in Dresden," she explained. "My people lived there, and did not leave until things got rather bad. They were not ill-treated, but thought it better to cross the frontier, as their health was beginning to suffer. Indeed, I lost both father and mother while we were in Geneva."

"Tough luck!"

"But why do we keep on discussing the mournful side of life? I feel quite gay, really. Perhaps, though, I shouldn't, because I have a horrid notion that Sir William is dead."

"By Jove! I believe you are right. I've thought so for some hours, but did not dare tell you."

Miss Bingham took this startling admission with surprising calmness.

"You see," she said confidentially, evidently pursuing her own line of thought, "he was mixed up with such queer people."

"Queer?"

"Well, 'dangerous' would be the better word. He was one of the most retiring men I have ever met, but he simply could not help talking about the particular branch of research in which be was engaged at the moment. Recently it was this gas you spoke of last night."

"Methane?"

"Yes. What exactly is it?"

"Marsh gas."

"Yes, I know. But can marsh gas be used in warfare?"

"It might be. I cannot say. I am no chemist."

"Evidently Sir William thought it could be made most deadly. Any nation which had exclusive control of a gas of the sort could subdue the rest of the world with incredible speed."

"I can hardly imagine anything more criminal."

"Criminal! I don't agree. If men must kill each other for the sake of power or a political theory, why not get the nasty business over and done with in a week rather than four years? Don't look so shocked. If we must talk about war, you may as well hear my honest opinion of it."

"You are reasoning on the higher place. You survey the earth and the midgets thereon from an Olympian standpoint."

Miss Bingham, who seemed to be enjoying a sole meunière, lifted her glass and gazed thought fully at the amber wine it held.

"Englishmen always talk lightly of great peril," she said. "Now, I know what I am talking about. I assure you, in all sincerity, that if I were convinced that Sir William had perfected his scheme and that, by some mischance, his secret had fallen into the hands of a foreign and hostile Power, I would be in America, North or South, as quickly as I could get there."

"Matters are as bad as that, eh? Well, I have ordered a péche Melba to follow the casserole. Then, if you like, I'll drive you to the Passport Office."

"I do wish you would be serious."

"Surely one can say even serious things with a smile."

"Ah, you mean the true word spoken in jest. Am I to take it that way?"

"If you wish."

"Then you know that Sir William is dead—that he was murdered last Tuesday? But why ask? You knew it when we met last evening. Why didn't you speak? You cannot possibly have imagined that I had anything to do with it?"

"I can go further, much further. I am quite sure of your innocence." And Mannering's tone was as grave now as even the inflexible Miss Bingham could desire. He was well aware of her deliberate intent. She was leading up to some dramatic disclosure, and it would be folly to thwart her by another flippant comment.

"But see what valuable time we have wasted," she went on, almost vindictively. "You have no idea of the gulf opening at our very feet. It can swallow any of us. You, I, those friends of yours in Yorkshire, if they were ever so remotely connected with my employer—we are all threatened."

"By what?"

Sudden and violent death."

"Great Scott! What have I done, for instance?"

"You have shown a too intimate acquaintance with the object of Sir William's visit to Yorkshire."

"But I don't know the first thing about it. Dash it all! If I had the formula for methane gas in my waistcoat pocket at this very instant, I could neither read it nor use it."

"That is not what is troubling me. If, as you put it, you had the formula in your pocket, I would ask you to destroy it and announce openly what you had done."

"Why not confide it to the care of the War Office?"

"And give England an overwhelming power denied to others?"

"She would not avail herself of it."

Miss Bingham allowed herself to laugh harshly.

"Tell that to Moscow or Berlin, and you will hear some caustic jibes," she said.

"But what's going to happen to us if either Moscow or Berlin gets hold of it first?"

"The very worst. Please don't regard me as an hysterical woman, Captain Mannering. If you know that the formula exists, and where it is to-day, I can give you some very sound advice."

"On my honour, I have no knowledge whatsoever of it."

"Well, our conversation has taken a quite exciting turn, hasn't it? May I have a little more wine?"

"I beg your pardon. I am a poor host, I fear. But, as you are so worried, I may be able to help a little. A friend of mine, Colonel Westoby, is—"

"Westoby!" she broke in. "He has written to Sir William many times."

"Possibly. He's in the India Office. At this moment he is seated not many tables away. Would you care to meet him? He must have the very latest information concerning Sandling and his doings."

"Oh yes. Take me to him!"

"Better still, I'll bring him here. Pardon me one minute."

In sober truth, Mannering was inwardly on fire. He had kept up a nerve-racking discussion, every sign of animated interest, yet his brain was analysing almost fiercely an affrighting theory. Was Betty Hardacre in immediate danger? Had the bolt fallen already? The German girl's candour was not simulated. She was telling the truth. Why? Because by that means alone could she hope to unlock his lips. All she wanted to know was what had become of the written record of Sir William Sandling's invention. Nothing else mattered. She could afford to let slip hints of the gravest import—hints which might well be transmuted into bitter facts within a few days or hours. Her position was unassailable. If questioned by the authorities, she could plead an altruistic regard for the public weal. Her close association with the greatest of British chemists, the visits to his house of all manner of foreign agents, his correspondence with various Government departments, the very secrecy in which he had cloaked his life during the past few weeks, and, finally, his death at the hands of assassins— these things, taken collectively, had opened her eyes to the dangers threatening the State as well as individuals. Mannering had not the least doubt that she could explain most plausibly the why and wherefore of her intimate acquaintance with recent events in Yorkshire. Mr. Winter himself had intimated that her actual German nationality would be difficult to prove. It may be taken for granted, therefore, that Mannering did some hard thinking during that casual stroll along a few feet of carpet in the Ritz Restaurant.

Westoby, of course, was surprised by his action, which was as well if other eyes were watching. He half rose, and introduced his companion—no less a person than Sir Herbert Bland, a member of the India Council.

"You two finished your luncheon?" began Mannering, forcing a conventional smile and speaking with the flippant unconcern of a young man about Town. He took for granted, of course, that both men were aware of Beatrice Bingham's identity.

"Nearly," said the Colonel.

"Well, my lady friend over there is desperately anxious to find out whether the formula was stolen in

Yorkshire on Tuesday or is now in safe custody in London. I told her, Westoby, that you might know, so I want you to come and have a chat with her."

"I?" was the wrathful demand. Such a request was the last thing he either expected or wished to comply with.

"Yes, you." And Mannering's desperate earnestness was strangely at variance with his unconcerned air. "Of course, you will not gratify her curiosity, but you literally must play up. I'll help. . . . I appeal to you, sir "—this to the other man—" to get in touch with Scotland Yard without one second's unnecessary delay, and tell them to phone their own representatives at Foxton, Yorkshire, or, failing them, Superintendent Dunkeld, the local chief of police, saying that Miss Hardacre is probably in real personal danger, and should be safeguarded most thoroughly. The only names you need remember are those two—Dunkeld and Hardacre. If I wait another instant I may arouse suspicion. Can I rely on you?"

"Naturally," said the man from the India Office, a K.C.S.I., K.C.I.E., and many other things.

"Good!" said Mannering, blissfully unaware of the offence with such patronising approval might convey. "Come along, Westoby! The lady waits!"

Luckily, his new ally was a resourceful fellow. He acted his part splendidly. After paying the bill without undue hurry, he sauntered out, waving a casual farewell to Westoby in passing. He even halted to light a cigarette at the exit before hailing a taxi and giving a Pall Mall club as his destination. Once en route, however, he bade the man rush him to Scotland Yard at top speed.

That was a wise decision. He not only saved time, but, in the result, was placed in direct communication with Dunkeld, from whom he learnt that Winter and Furneaux had left Foxton for London that morning.

The superintendent treated Mannering' s warning with due seriousness. He thought, however, that Miss Hardacre was safe enough at the moment.

"To the best of my belief," he said, "she is busy now with a batch of cablegrams and correspondence in the doctor's house. A constable is on duty a few yards away, because a fair was held in our small town during the past three days, and there is always the possibility that some members of the gang responsible for Sir William Sandling's death may be lurking among the riff raff which gathered in the wake of this as of every other caravan crowd. The regular show-men are decent fellows, but they depend to some extent on casual labour. Is Captain Mannering all right?"

"Oh yes, you can bank on that," laughed the member of the Council. "I have just come from the Ritz, where he was lunching with the fascinating Miss Bingham."

"Ah! Furneaux will attend to her pretty soon, I imagine. Her right place is in the laundry of one of His Majesty's prisons."

"A pity, superintendent. She's a good looker!"

She would be of little use for her job otherwise, Sir Herbert. Yet there cannot be the slightest doubt that she is a skilful and unscrupulous international spy— whatever that may mean after what we read of European harmony at Locarno."

"So there are cynics up in Yorkshire?"

"Well, we cannot bring ourselves to believe that any sensible politician does owt for nowt when it comes to a deal. Can you follow our language?"

"Can a duck swim? I was born and bred in Swaledale, where, I suppose, I am forgotten, seeing that my father was only a moor-edge farmer."

"I'm sorry, Sir Herbert. Our county produces so many great men that it is difficult to keep track of them all."

"Oh, is that so? Mannering should have told me you were a champion leg-puller! Well, I asked for it, and got it. One of these days I'll drop in on you at Foxton and discuss the point. Meanwhile – "

"One moment!"

Dunkeld's pleasantly modulated accents had suddenly sharpened to a note of anger or anxiety—it was hard to say which—but the man at the other end of the wire two hundred miles away knew well that the emphatic request for silence had nothing whatever to do with the trivial and amusing turn their talk had taken. Never before, during a long and varied official life, had he been so acutely conscious of the singular difference between the mere cessation of conversation over a connected telephone and the sheer deadness of negation when contact is broken. He felt now that he was actually in the presence of a man keyed up to a tense alertness which bespoke unforeseen and imminent danger.

Sir Herbert nodded to the inspector who had received him at headquarters.

"Take that second receiver," he whispered. "Something sensational is going on at Foxton at this very minute."

Nor was he mistaken. In a few seconds the superintendent's voice came again, and there was a snap in it this time.

"I hear shooting at the other end of the village," he said. "You at the Yard? Well, stand fast, and I'll call you again as quickly as possible!"

Then the two hundred miles intervened. "This is a pretty rotten business," growled Sir Herbert.

Somehow, mainly because of his complete helplessness be felt inclined to blame himself for not having hurried away from the restaurant. If only he could retrieve those wasted moments of needless play-acting!

"I can't even guess what is happening, sir," said the C.I.D. man, "but there is no reason for alarm, because Mr. Dunkeld has rushed out. If somebody is shooting, it means that the police are busy, whatever the result may be. Did you see Mr. Sheldon at the Ritz?"

No. I wouldn't know him if I had seen him. And what can he do, or any of us? Damn it all! this girl they speak so well of may be lying dead in that village street, all

because I tried to hood wink some infernal German
woman who was too much taken up with Captain
Mannering to have eyes for anybody else!"

Wherein, as shall be seen, the member of Council did
himself less than justice. The youngest and most cocksure
dramatist writing unwholesome "thrillers" for the English
stage to-day could not have devised a more striking
"curtain" than that now dropping on a scene in real life,
set most convincingly in the centre of Foxton's market-
place! But it was not to be controlled from London. For
weal or woe, its denouement was entrusted irrevocably to
the capable hands of Superintendent Dunkeld.

CHAPTER 10: FOXTON WAKES UP

THE superintendent cut short his talk with Sir Herbert Bland because a single shot from an automatic pistol, followed by two more in quick succession, had come from that end of the village where Dr. Lysaght's house lay. Those versed in the use of modern firearms find little, if any, difficulty in differentiating between the sounds of a rifle, a shotgun, and a high-velocity pistol. Dunkeld had good reason to believe that the constable on guard near the doctor's house possessed the only weapon in Foxton at that moment which gave the true automatic snarl. That is to say, it should be the only one if the law of the land were obeyed; consequently, no recognised inhabitant of the little town itself other than the policeman could be the offender.

Dunkeld belonged to the rare order of executive officer who follows the excellent advice of the Roman sage that a leader should hasten slowly. He wasted no valuable seconds by gazing out of the windows, because his office did not command an extensive view of the main street on the side which mattered. He was alone. All his men were engaged elsewhere in some task directly connected with the search for the murderers of Sir William Sandling. He was unarmed, his own revolver having gone to swell the armament which might possibly be needed during the scouring of the countryside. But when duty gave a few free hours he liked to take an afternoon's stroll with a gun and walk up the mixed bag which stubble, pasture, and gorse will yield. So, as he passed swiftly through the hall, he snatched a 12-bore from its rack and grabbed a handful of cartridges out of a bag hanging on a nearby peg, the whole equipment having been put there quite recently in readiness for the shooting season.

He was not surprised at finding the street free from any real commotion. Foxton had just endured a three-days' orgy of shooting galleries, steam organs, and shrill whistles, so the communal mind had not yet gone back to that normal state of placidity when an outburst of pistol-shots would have brought out of doors everyone not absolutely bedridden.

He, of course, was under no delusion in the matter. Not only did he recognise the probable origin of the firing, but he was, so to speak, subconsciously prepared for it by the warning telephoned from London a few seconds earlier. As a consequence, he was all eyes for the unusual, the bizarre. He would have disregarded a drove of cattle being stampeded by a trio of racing charabancs, but he did not fail to interpret correctly the swift approach of a closed car, the chase of the said car by a frenzied fox-terrier, and the presence of an unhelmeted and seemingly disabled policeman in the midst of a small group of townsfolk gathered on the road in front of the Lysaght residence.

They were all gazing after the fleeting car, and the policeman was not so thoroughly knocked out as to be unable to signal his chief that the fugitives must be stopped. Nor was the promise of help altogether lacking. A butcher ran out from his shop carrying a useful-looking cleaver. A goggled motor-cyclist, who had halted for a moment apparently to ascertain from the gesticulating constable what all the fuss was about, was bowling along now in hot pursuit. At the moment the latter came on the scene the car was about fifty yards from the superintendent, while the cyclist had only just detached himself from the men in the middle of the road two hundred yards farther away.

The thoroughfare, an unusually wide one for a country town, ran due north and south, and the car was heading north. At that hour, about two o'clock by Act of Parliament, but one o'clock according to the sun's reckoning, the interior of the car was completely in the shadow. The windscreen was tilted at such an angle that it would have been almost impossible to discern the occupants were the pace a mere crawl; at a round mile in each minute and a half they became a blur. And, in exactly two and a half seconds they would whirl past! Luckily, however, Dunkeld had already decided to take a tremendous chance and shoot to kill if his summons to halt were not obeyed, or, at any rate, if the engine were not shut off and the brakes applied.

This experienced officer of police knew well what he risked if he erred. Public opinion, that fickle and irresponsible element in human affairs, is so accustomed to the guardians of British law and order acting correctly at all times that the thousand cases where the police protect the community by judicious action are never taken into account when the one instance comes along wherein an innocent person suffers. In effect, if anyone in that flying car were shot dead or even dangerously wounded because the driver fumbled with his levers, and it was proved that no evil motive inspired such a burst of speed, Dunkeld would be lucky indeed if he escaped a worse fate than compulsory retirement from the service with resultant loss of pension.

Of course, being the sort of man he was, he did not hesitate for any appreciable part of the two and a half seconds at his disposal. Holding the gun in his left hand he held out his right, and even shouted loudly the one word: "Stop!"

The man at the wheel answered by pressing on the accelerator, and Dunkeld caught a glimpse of a wicked-looking muzzle being thrust beneath the movable wind-screen. He stepped smartly sideways, and a bullet crashed against the wall of a house behind him but higher up the road. Simultaneously Dunkeld raised his 12-bore and fired at the glass shield. It was not in human nature that the driver, unless he were a trained soldier, taught from military infancy that attack is the best defence, should not endeavour to swerve away from rather than toward the imminent peril, so the superintendent's first barrel literally swept the upper parts of the bodies of two men on the front seat. The car continued its swerve, mounted a cobbled pavement which bounded the road, hit a coster's barrow, and swung completely round. It was only saved from turning over by the radiator being forced into the porch of a Georgian house. By this time both front tyres had burst and a rear wheel had buckled.

Dunkeld saw that the men in front were out of action. Indeed, the automatic pistol which began this second phase of the battle had bounced off the bonnet and fallen clear, since the No. 6 shot from the 12-bore had made a sad mess of its owner's right hand. But there were others in the closed limousine, so the superintendent, who refused to be shot down at the very moment success was in sight, raised his gun again in readiness to forestall any renewed offensive.

"Don't shoot!" came a shrill and singularly clear voice. "Miss Hardacre's in there!"

The motor-cyclist had arrived, and was dismounting in a highly effective way by running the front wheel alongside the disabled car and swinging his inner leg clear. Moreover, he produced an automatic, and evidently meant using it if necessary.

"Stand clear of me and I'll open the door," he cried. "There are two men holding the girl. I'll take care of anyone who makes trouble on this side—you might watch out that no one gets away through the other door, as this small burg is full of alleys and backyards."

"That's all right, Mr. Furneaux," agreed Dunkeld, speaking with equal coolness. "I don't imagine that these fellows will fight now, and Mr. Thompson "—the butcher with the cleaver—"will knock the block off any idiot who tries to pass him."

Thompson signified in the vernacular that he would an' all. By this time, too, a score of others were ready to help.

Furneaux, meanwhile, had torn open the door, no mean feat for so small a man, because it was badly jammed and the hinges were displaced.

"Now, out you come!" he cried. "And step lively, too! This box of tricks will be on fire at any moment. . . . Hello, Pierre! "—this to an undersized, swarthy fellow, a villainous caricature of Furneaux himself, who sprang out nimbly. "Nom de Dieu! I thought you had more wit than to mix yourself up with these imbeciles! Got him, superintendent? Let two of your strong-armed friends catch hold till we can attend to the whole gang. . . . Well, well! Now see who's here! Big Doolan himself, only a week back from Moscow! . . . Oh, dash it all! Call your dog off, Miss Hardacre!"

Tags had dashed through the crowd, and, without any display of uncertainty or hesitation, had caused his front teeth to meet in Big Doolan's right hand. The man was hardly to blame if in his pain and fury he tried to kill a valiant assailant, but there were those present who knew how to deal with a situation of that sort, so Tags was rescued, and held back from further reprisal or mischief, which was as well, because his earlier enemy, the Yorkshire terrier from the White Horse Inn, had just arrived, and was so eager for the fray that he could not bark, but emitted a shrill yelp which seemed to be squeezed out of his small body by each onward spring.

Betty did not stir, nor could she speak, though her eyes were smiling bravely. She had been trussed in a sort of harness of leather and canvas, which comprised a gag, firmly secured over the top of her head, under her chin, and round her neck, and straps round her waist and arms buckled to an iron rod attached to the back of the car; it had, in fact, been put there that morning for the purpose.

The detective soon set her free, though with not a second to spare, for petrol from a burst tank was seeping along the rough pavement to a nearly red-hot exhaust pipe. In the event, Betty just missed the first rush of flame, while Dunkeld and his helpers were barely able to

lift the injured men free from the front seat before the car
was well ablaze. Of course, there were chemical
extinguishers and sand available, and the fire was
mastered speedily. Not that it mattered a great deal. The
gears were all smashed, the cylinders dislodged, and the
whole frame work twisted. Even the most enthusiastic
second hand dealer must have admitted in this instance
that it would be cheaper to buy a new car than repair the
old one.

Furneaux's first concern was for Betty.

"Sure you're not hurt?" he inquired, when she could
stand by his side well clear of the bonfire.

Not in the least," she answered. "Angry, yes, because I
was such a zany as to believe that Dr. Lysaght had sent
for me in a hurry. For the rest, I was too surprised to
offer any real resistance. That man whom you addressed
as Doolan humbugged me completely. He rang the front
door bell, told the maid he had a message for me from the
doctor, who, I knew, had been called away by phone to an
accident at a farm some miles out in the country—"

She broke off suddenly when Furneaux clicked his
tongue in a peculiar way.

"Why, of course "she cried wrathfully. "I see the whole
scheme now! The doctor will be back at any moment in a
furious temper because there has been no accident – "

"Never mind, Miss Hardacre. We have arranged to
keep him busy here for an hour or more. Please go on!
Every second is valuable."

"Well, this Doolan, a rather fawning, plausible fellow
when he wants to be agreeable, said there was a
gentleman in the waiting car who could explain matters
fully. It simply did not occur to me that there could be
any danger in broad daylight, with a policeman standing
a few yards away. Why, the main street itself begins at
that very spot! So, followed by Tags, I crossed the
pavement, Doolan opened the door, and I was instantly
thrust inside, falling on my knees. I heard Tags yelp as
though he had been kicked. Then there was some

shooting, and while I was being buckled to the seat and a gag thrust into my mouth the car started. What is it all about? What have I done that I should be kidnapped in this fashion?"

"Please tell Mrs. Lysaght I'll be along for a cup of tea about four o'clock. Then I'll explain to-day's excitement. By the way, I'm inclined to believe that you are safe now from any further attack. I didn't expect that this one would be made quite so soon. . . . Yes, a cryptic remark, as you would say. But you must bide a wee. Can you walk back to the doctor's house? The man carrying Tags will go with you."

"Walk? I'm not crippled, if that is what you mean. But, really—mayn't I have a pistol or a dagger for self-defence?"

"Take mine! You won't need it, but—if it will make you feel happier—" Furneaux affected to treat her seriously, and produced the automatic which he had pocketed. But Betty only laughed.

"No, no!" she said. "One never knows who may be looking. What a delightful story it would be for to-morrow's Leeds newspapers: 'Miss Betty Hardacre, soon after she was rescued from the burning car, passed along the Foxton High Street carrying a revolver, and was evidently prepared to use it on the least provocation.' My hat! I would never hear the last of it in the Common Room at the College. But, must I go at once? This affair is just becoming interesting."

"You're perfectly admirable!" admitted the detective. "Follow the prisoners into Mr. Dunkeld's office and tell him I sent you. I'll give this brace of winged birds the once-over before I join the committee. . . Oh, here comes the superintendent himself, so you had better wait."

Dunkeld had merely seen to the handcuffing and superficial searching of Pierre and Doolan before leaving them in the care of Thompson, the butcher, and others who had acted as special constables during the war years. The two bandits had yielded four pistols and a dozen

packets of ammunition. In the conditions it was
remarkable that they did not show fight, but the
destruction of the car was probably the chief factor. They
could not have escaped. Had they resisted capture, they
might have lost their own lives forthwith, while their
fate, if they killed anyone, must be what is known to the
law as *res judicata.*

Foxton boasted an ambulance unit, and of its
members were doing their best to bind shattered hand
and lacerated shoulder of the fellow who had fired at
Dunkeld. He was delirious with pain, and Furneaux alone
knew that he was muttering imprecations in Russian.

The chauffeur, too, had come off badly. Pellets had
lodged in his jaws, neck, and chest. Possibly none of the
punctures would prove fatal, but he was in for a most
unpleasant experience when some eminent surgeon had
him on an operating table and began demonstrating to a
score of watchful students the correct treatment of
gunshot wounds. Dr. Lysaght, whirling into Foxton like a
thunder-cloud, approved the work of his class, and saw to
it that two such excellent cases were not wasted on the
nearest cottage hospital; he despatched them to Leeds.
The extra journey was uncomfortable for the patients, but
most beneficial to the medical school of the University.

Furneaux and Dunkeld ascertained quickly enough
that this precious pair were mere hirelings. The only
important item was the identification of the gunman by
the constable who had been told off to mount guard over
Betty. He was practically uninjured. He had seen the car
halt in front of the doctor's house, and watched Doolan
make a leisurely statement to the young lady when she
appeared. That she should be bundled into the limousine
so unceremoniously, however, was a different matter. He
ran forward, whipped out his pistol, and fired at the off
front tyre when the engine started. He missed, but hit a
spoke of the rear artillery wheel, thus contributing to its
collapse later. In response, the specialist seated by the
driver's side leaned out and aimed at the policeman's

upper works. The direction was accurate, but the elevation faulty. The bullet sent the policeman's helmet flying and ploughed a slight furrow along the centre of his scalp. The blow was hard enough to knock its recipient off his feet, which was fortunate, because a second shot struck the road some feet in rear of the spot where he was lying.

For a few minutes, of course, all Foxton was a prey to excitement and confusion. It was discovered, for instance, that Mrs. Dunkeld, looking out from a bedroom window, had witnessed the brief duel between her husband and the desperadoes in the car. When it was over she fell in a faint. A servant heard the shooting, followed by the thud of her mistress's body on a carpeted floor, and rushed out screaming that the "missus" had been shot. The burning car, too, set fire to some woodwork in the Georgian porch. During the resultant scurry with a hose someone trod heavily on the fore-paws of the Yorkshire terrier, whose shrieks of anguish were heart-rending.

All this, especially the part played by Tags's foe, Furneaux described callously as "comic relief."

"If I had not actually seen the wretched whelp," he added, "I would never have believed that one small dog could make so much noise. And he seemed to blame Tags for his injuries. Within a minute he was sitting on Dunkeld's door step, waiting for the other warrior to appear."

At last, however, order was restored. The wreck of the car was dragged into the stable-yard of the inn, and the two wounded prisoners were laid out on stretchers in the charge-room of the police station. Then Dunkeld and Furneaux took Betty and her dog to the room where the uninjured captives were seated.

Pierre Girard, a southern Frenchman by birth, and partly Spanish by descent, looked sulky and thoroughly out of conceit with life, but Doolan, to whom Betty had applied the right adjective, was actually trying to ingratiate himself with the stolid Yorkshiremen who held

him in charge. His attitude changed at once, however,
when the girl came in. He had his own reasons for
knowing that she would show him no mercy.

Furneaux, of course, needed no enlightenment on this
point. He saw how Betty's eyes hardened at sight of the
man, and noted the expression of genial truculence fade
from her captor's face. It was typical of the little
detective's innate chivalry that he sought no explanation,
yet, from that instant, Big Doolan's chance of saving his
own skin by incriminating others vanished utterly.

"We have no use for this Bolshie from Cork," he said
to Dunkeld in a contemptuous undertone. "Can't you lock
him up in a cell till it is decided what is to be done with
him? Charge him with aggravated assault and attempted
murder, and have him thoroughly searched. You should
have plenty of reinforcements here before you are ready
to put him away."

"Reinforcements?" The superintendent raised his
eyebrows. "Where from?"

"Malton, Pickering, Kirbymoorside. The Chief
Constable at York promised to phone your headquarters.
Of course, this is all Greek to you. Winter and I had a
half-hour's wait at York, so we gave the Yard a call, and
were told that these four lads had arrived in
Middlesbrough this morning from London. That was
enough. While I arranged for the hire of a motor-cycle
and disguised myself as a speed merchant, Winter saw
the York police, and they ascertained from
Middlesbrough that the gang had gone openly to a garage
and secured a reliable car by leaving a deposit as well as
full rates for a hundred miles run. They explained that
they were touring the country to pick up greyhounds for
racing purposes. I suppose you can guess the remainder
of the story for the time being?"

A car stopped in the street outside. Dunkeld was near
a window.

"Here are five able-bodied policemen," he said. "Give
me as many minutes, and I'll be with you. For half that

time I really must see to my wife, who nearly faded away when the row began. I forgot that she was in the room overhead. . . . Come along, Doolan! You'll be able to walk in those leg-irons if you watch your step."

The big man rose. He was in a towering rage, but he said no word. He knew, too, that at the least sign of resistance his right wrist would be nearly broken by a special appliance designed for that very purpose. Nor did Tags forget to growl a farewell.

"C'est mieux, n'est-ce pas?" said Furneaux to Girard when Doolan had gone.

"What, then, does it matter to me, this?" answered the other in his own language.

The detective shrugged his shoulders. He turned to Betty.

"I take it that Pierre did not offer you any indignity?" he said.

"No. He did not hurt me at all," she declared.

"He wouldn't. You see, he was born a gentleman. In fact, if he hadn't been compelled to be extraordinarily good when young, he would not be so extraordinarily bad to-day."

Betty giggled; there is no other name for it. Butcher Thompson and the farmers in the room may have grinned later—be it remembered that they had not the least notion as to the identity of this little wisp of a man in overalls and goggles who so coolly assumed command of everyone and everything in Foxton, if not in the whole North of England—but the Frenchman smiled cynically. He, at least, felt the truth of the epigram.

Suddenly the detective's attention was given to the departure of some visitors from the White Horse. A touring car had appeared from a neighbouring garage, a couple of portmanteaux were placed in it, and two men, each carrying a square box covered with rainproof canvas, took their seats and drove off rapidly southwards.

Furneaux turned to Dunkeld, who entered at that moment, being in need of a duplicate key for the cells.

"I suppose the place is overrun flow with special correspondents?" he said sharply.

"Yes. They have been bothering me all the morning, but I packed them off to Blackdown. Why not?"

"Including the camera-men?"

"What camera-men?"

"The two who have just scooted out of the inn."

"I did not even know they were there."

"Sacre' nom d'un nom! Do you hear that, Pierre? And you, Miss Hardacre? You, I, all of us are in the movies. We have just given the motion picture industry its first genuine thrill—motor bandits, pretty girl, gallant policeman, faithful hound, abduction, rescue, real shooting, with a perfect setting and a crowd of first-rate supers. And in staid old England, too, of all places in the world. . . . Look! That pair of babies opened both windows on the first floor of the White Horse. The shots exchanged outside the doctor's house gave them sufficient warning to get ready and focus their machines at landscape distance. Oh, what a story! I'll bet you an even sixpence, Dunkeld, they will even show your wife fainting at the upper window. And they'll have every name pat except mine! I shall figure as an unknown but plucky motor cyclist. *O là, là!* We shall all be famous from China to Peru!"

The superintendent said nothing. He merely lifted a key off a hook and went out. Fully half an hour later, while discussing the affair quietly with the little detective, he remarked that there would have been no real difficulty in overtaking the photographers, or, at any rate, in having them intercepted between Foxton and York.

Furneaux was nearly caught—nearly, but not quite. He was just able to stop the retort that trembled on his lips. As it was, he cackled derisively.

"I get your point!" he chirped. "You regarded this as an occasion when the uniformed police might fairly be given a show?"

"Far be it from me to suggest that Scotland Yard usually mops up most of the limelight!" smiled Dunkeld.

"There's treason in the thought! Next time I'll run you down first, and then plug in a shot or two on my own. Wait till you see the picture, and you'll realise how I left the centre of the stage to you and Tags. I'm accustomed to such ingratitude in London, but it's appalling to find it rampant in the provinces!"

Chapter 11: Drawing the Coverts

"THE Eternal Triangle," that unfailing recipe for the plot of a motion picture, proved a ghastly failure when put to the test of everyday life with Miss Beatrice Bingham as the woman and Mannering and Colonel Westoby as the men during the second half of the luncheon at the Ritz. Indeed, Sir Herbert Bland was hardly in touch with Dunkeld by phone before the lady they were discussing announced that she must return to Welbeck Street at once and alone.

She so evidently meant what she said that Mannering did not attempt to dissuade her. Within a minute she was in a taxi and gone. The Colonel, a married man who probably had never given a thought to any woman other than his wife, was somewhat disconcerted.

"I'm afraid I don't understand the ways of the modern girl," he said apologetically when he and Mannering came together again for a cigarette and a liqueur. "I tried to play up, but, honestly, I don't think your young friend listened to a word I said. What went wrong?"

Mannering laughed.

"Well, for one thing," he grinned, "you're an uncommonly poor liar, sir."

"Dash it all, even if I had the inclination, what was I to lie about?"

"Oh, scores of topics—the anxiety of the War Office about Sandling's death, the increasing strain of the international position, the effect on the rest of the world of a sudden and ruthless use of a devastating gas by the nation which first discovers it and is able to manufacture large quantities in secret."

"Do you call that lying? I regard each item you have mentioned as a bitter and vital truth."

"Exactly. That is why a sensitive and highly trained intelligence like Fraulein Bertha's would have realised at once that you were saying these things to lead her on, and, in consequence, not have believed you."

The older man shook his head.

"I don't follow metaphysical reasoning of that sort," he growled. "If you want my candid opinion I can give it without any word-twisting. I don't know what mood you left her in, but she was thoroughly upset and suspicious when we rejoined her."

Mannering was well aware of this, but he had long ago seen the unwisdom of anticipating discoveries or deductions which might be made by a senior officer with whom he was working, or whose good services he might need later.

"Oh, you think that, do you, sir?" he inquired, modestly receptive of so much sagacity.

"Yes, and I'll go one better by telling you what happened. If Scotland Yard has some of its agents in this room they will probably bear out my guess that the moment you quitted Miss Bingham she received some sort of signal from three men at a table almost directly behind me but at the other side of the restaurant. Bland and I spotted them the moment they came in. One is a square-head—the others genuine Slavs. Our London tailors are true democrats, but they cannot change the shape of their customers' skulls or the angle of their cheek-bones."

"Good for you, Colonel!" cried Mannering. "But I, too, must plead guilty to being a disturbing influence. I was getting along fine with the fair Bertha until it dawned on me that some of the pests who knocked poor old Sandling on the head might possibly suspect Betty Hardacre of having a knowledge of the formula. Obviously, they'll stop at nothing to secure it if it has been set forth in black and white."

"Well, I may as well tell you now that it has. It will even be tested on a small scale in the Long Valley this afternoon."

"I'm sorry to hear that. Couldn't the authorities have waited? Why advertise such a discovery?"

"Advertise it? Who will know of it outside a most confidential circle? Hang it all, we must trust somebody."

"All the same, I wish the practical experiments could have been deferred."

"But, my dear fellow, I happen to be aware of some of the arrangements. A cavalry brigade is to be trained in 'screen' work, starting from Laffan's Plain half an hour before the gas is liberated and fired. No unauthorised person can possibly get within a mile of the place from this very moment onwards."

Westoby verified the time, two o'clock. He would not have been quite so sure of his ground if he knew what was happening just then in Foxton High Street, which, for comparison, might be regarded as far less likely to attract the attention of foreign spies than the principal training centre of the British Army.

"Probably you are right," agreed Mannering, anxious to avoid even the semblance of criticism. "To tell the honest truth," he added, "I have not yet quite got over last night's uncanny sensation of sitting with one's back to a concealed enemy. I'm aware of it again now. Maybe one of the three lads you have spotted here was the gentleman hidden behind the curtain in Welbeck Street. . . . Well, well; who'd have thought at the beginning of this week that you and I would be up to the neck in the old game once more? Do you remember that night in a Chin Lushai valley when you and I were stretched out in the wet jungle, watching a meeting between that son of a gun, Weng Chu, and those silly asses, the headmen of a group of villages at the entrance to the Bhamo District?"

Westoby wriggled uneasily.

"What a reminiscence to bring to mind after a good luncheon!" he protested. "The leeches were bad enough. But that infernal snake! I I can feel it yet—can you?"

"I felt it first," sniggered the younger man. "I took jolly good care to press close to you so that the blighter couldn't get his head up. I've often wondered what kind of snake it was. It may have been a perfectly harmless one."

"And it may not. To me all snakes are rank poison. It's queer you should have mentioned that. The passing of the wretched thing saved Weng Chu's life—at any rate, gave a respite. I resolved at once that if the snake got me, I would get him—Weng, I mean. It was quite a relief when the rascal was shot in fair fight a few days later. . . . But this won't do. I have a heap of work waiting. Shall I see you at dinner to-night?"

"If I am free. There may be constabulary duty to be done, and for the time being I must obey orders, I suppose."

Mannering did not think it necessary to explain more fully that the breakdown of the luncheon might have been due quite as much to his own strange behaviour as to any hint or command Sir William's secretary received from one of her cosmopolitan associates. He had suddenly conceived a violent and wholly irrational hatred of her. He could not even tolerate her propinquity. It seemed hardly credible that an hour earlier he had squeezed her arm when they were together in the taxi.

Nevertheless, being an eminently sane person, he did not permit morbid notions of that sort to dominate him.

"What I want is exercise," he decided, so there and then he set off down Piccadilly and did the complete round of Hyde Park and Kensington Gardens at a spanking pace.

On reaching the club he fell asleep, and did not wake up until a valet entered to lay out his dress clothes. He was changing when the telephone rang and the hall porter announced: "Mr. Wilkins to see you, sir."

For an instant Mannering was puzzled. Then, luckily, he associated the name with the Welbeck Street house.

"Send him up," he said. "He won't mind having a chat while I finish dressing."

A glance at the butler's worried face showed that something alarming had happened during the afternoon. Wilkins had been an anxious man at the lunch hour— now he was a thoroughly frightened one. He wore the conventional outdoor garb of his craft, a spotless but rather threadbare black morning coat and waistcoat and dark striped trousers. He carried one of those singularly shaped bowler hats fashioned like a truncated cone, which seem to be made for butlers and farm bailiffs and purchasable by them alone. Mannering noticed that some newspapers had been stuffed into the interior.

"Well, sir, this is a nice how-d'ye-do – " he began, but Mannering lifted a hand and recalled the bell-boy who had brought the visitor upstairs.

"A whisky and soda or a stiff cocktail?" he inquired.

The butler admitted he could "do with a bracer," which, it appeared, was a "gin and mixed."

"And what has gone wrong now?" said Mannering airily, since he did not know yet how far he could take the man into his confidence.

"Everything, sir," came the surprising statement, and Wilkins practically collapsed into the armchair. "The guv'nor's been dead these two days an' more, it would seem, an' Miss Bingham is just doing a bunk to Holland by way of Harwich, an' some other young lady whom I've never heard of before, though the papers say she's Sir William's secretary, has been kidnapped by motor bandits in some little town up in Yorkshire."

"What's that?" growled Mannering, and such lightnings blazed from his eyes that the butler wilted visibly.

"Here, hold on, sir!" he gasped. "You ain't blamin' me, are you? You asked me to come and see you, and I jumped at the chance, because no real white man has called at Sir

William's house during the past three weeks. I came as soon as I could."

"Yes, yes. But what is this about the kidnapping of a young lady?"

"It's all in the evening papers, sir. Here you are. I've brought two."

Mannering could not wait even to open the proffered sheets.

"Is the lady's name mentioned? Is she a Miss Betty Hardacre?" he said, and Wilkins was not so unhinged as to be deaf to the dismay in the younger man's voice.

"Yes, sir. That's it—Miss Hardacre!" he wheezed. "But, bless your heart, sir, don't you worry—she's all right! Behaved like a brick, she did. You'll be able to see it all in the movies to-morrow evenin', the paper says."

Mannering, aware only of an almost overwhelming relief at the man's assurance as to Betty's well-being, gave slight heed to that concluding statement. He heard the words clearly enough, it is true, but dismissed them as some queer jumble of fact and fiction.

But he was quickly undeceived. The men who write up sensational news for the evening Press do not beat about the bush. They tell their story at once in glaring headlines and sharp, incisive sentences. And here was a case where the motion-picture operators who witnessed the shooting affray in Foxton High Street were themselves on the journalistic side of their profession. They had no need to depend on hearsay evidence. They described what they had actually seen and photographed.

It was an epic story, which lost none of its. savour because of the promise that the whole exciting and unprecedented episode—unprecedented, that is, as a cinematographic record of any such happening in real life—would be shown on the screen next day in many of the leading picture houses in London and the provinces.

There could be no gainsaying the accuracy of the double-leaded paragraphs in the large type of real display. The writers told bow they had gone on the moor early in the morning and taken pictures of the farm and its surroundings. Returning to Foxton for lunch they were debating the pros and cons of securing any further story in a quiet little town which could hardly yield any additional material for their "News Gazette "—they had already filmed Betty, Dr. Lysaght, and Superintendent Dunkeld—when the first shots of the battle brought them to the windows.

Thenceforth they had missed nothing. Owing to the importance of the affair, and Sir William Sandling's high place in the scientific world, special "announcers" would attend when the picture was displayed and elucidate its points and leading characters.

It did not take long for Mannering to grasp what all this meant, though he was far from guessing the identity of the motor-cyclist who arrived on the scene in the nick of time and behaved with such phenomenal coolness and courage.

"Have you been in communication with the police?" he demanded, whirling round suddenly on the dejected butler, who, of course, had his own reasons for lamenting the death of a generous employer.

"No, sir. What's the use?" was the unexpected answer.

"Every use in the world! You must tell them everything you know. This affair goes far beyond a mere outbreak of robbery, even though accompanied by murder."

"The police know all that I know and a lot more," persisted Wilkins. "I'm not exactly blind, and I soon found out that detectives were watching our place for weeks from the consulting-room of a doctor's house opposite. I couldn't make out what it was all about, but, of course, I said nothing to nobody, but I did think these past few days it would be as well if I kep' a sort of diary showing what people called and who they wanted, and that sort of thing. They were all foreigners. Believe me, sir, you're the first Englishman to come near us for a fortnight. An',

Miss Bingham, now—she's queer—not quite one of our folk, sir."

"Forgive me for seeming to be rude, Wilkins, but while I am putting through a call to Scotland Yard I want you to answer a few questions briefly. When Miss Bingham returned to-day at two o'clock, what did she do?"

"She was busy on the phone for a good hour or more."

"And then what?"

"Three men called separately but they all went out together—the young woman as well, I mean. That would be about four-thirty, but I couldn't get here at five, as my orders were to stand fast in case I was wanted."

"For what?"

"I didn't know then, sir, but I do now. I had to help to pack, or, at any rate, cord boxes of books and papers, which seemed to be all ready. Miss Bingham just threw her own few things together, anyhow. Of course, most of her belongings would be at her lodgings. She told me to say in reply to any inquiries that she would be back to-morrow, but I doubt it very much, sir—first, because she has taken a lot of stuff which, I am sure, is not hers, and, second, she had not been gone many minutes when the steamer people rang up from Harwich to say they were reserving four berths for to-night on the boat leaving for the Hook of Holland."

Mannering held up a warning hand. Sheldon was on the wire.

"Quite a coincidence "said the detective, in the even, unflurried voice which forbade panic and even seemed to chide impatience. "I was just about to try and get hold of you. I want you to start for the North at eleven p.m."

"For Foxton?" broke in Mannering eagerly.

"No. Not Foxton. That little town will be quiet now during the remainder of the century. You've seen the evening papers, of course?"

"Sir William's butler has just brought them. He is here now—in my room at the club."

"Ah, that's all right. Tell him he can go home and sleep soundly to-night."

"But he has a sort of dossier which you ought to see."

"No hurry. I'll look in on him in the morning. Mr. Winter has just turned up, and he is as interested as you in the news from Yorkshire. He was sure something dramatic would happen, but, of course, Furneaux must put the lid on a boiling pot by turning up the way he did."

"Was Furneaux the motor-cyclist?"

"Of course! You don't imagine that the average joy-rider is going to sail into any row so cheerfully where lead is flying from shotguns and automatics?"

"I don't feel like exercising my imagination in any shape or form at the moment. If I did, I might wonder why Miss Betty Hardacre was exposed to such damnable risk and very real ill-treatment."

"Now, Mr. Mannering. The Yard has not done badly in this case, as you will soon find out, but our men cannot be everywhere. I can't explain over the phone—"

"What about the butler, Mr. Wilkins?"

"Drat the fellow! Is he there still? Give him a drink and send him home."

"But he says—"

"That the party from the Ritz is bound for Harwich a the Continong? Yes. That's all right. They won't cross the grey North Sea for some days, if ever. Now, please listen! If you've dressed for dinner, change back to that nice blue serge which suits you so well. Then meet the Chief and me at eight o'clock at the Ristorante Milano - Proprietor V. Pucci—all of which is set forth in coloured lights at the top of Dean Street, Soho. Walk straight upstairs and enter the second room on the left, first floor. If anyone challenges you, the password for the week is 'Il Duce.' You will be given a far better dinner than at the club—"

"I've half promised to meet Westoby—"

"Can you trust him?"

"Trust Westoby. What on earth—?"

"Oh, I don't mean high treason. He's a departmental chief, or on the staff, anyhow, and those fellows sniff at unrecognised methods."

"Not Westoby, on your life. Great Scott! I'll get him to open up on 'the ordeal of the inflated goatskin,' as invented by him and practiced on various scoundrels in Assam and Burma."

"Is that so? You remember, I thought him rather chesty. Well, bring him, too."

"And where do I go afterwards?"

"A long way beyond Foxton. Really."

"Righto! See you at eight!"

Mannering did not want to hurt the butler's feelings by an abrupt dismissal, so he decided to use him.

"Look here," he said cheerily, "we're all in this business up to the neck. Will you give me a hand?"

"Certainly, sir," said Wilkins.

"Well, I'm going to put through a long distance call, and I have to change and rush out. If I chuck a few things on the bed, will you pack them for me?"

The man was delighted to help. He was an expert packer, too. He had nearly completed. his task when "Foxton 20" was announced. It was Lysaght who spoke, and he promptly dished Mannering's hope of exchanging a few words with Betty by saying that she was in bed and well dosed with bromide.

"Has she cracked up, then?" Mannering forced himself to say calmly.

"No. Indeed, she is rather sore with me for insisting on soup and sleep. But the feminine nervous organism in good health is like a violin in perfect tune. It will not suffer from use, but it certainly cannot stand a heavy bang. Now, Miss Hardacre had to endure a perfectly hellish couple of minutes this morning, and such a rough experience, coming after the insensibly severe strain of the past few days, means exhaustion. Of course, she'll deny it, yet I'm sure she'll be rather big-eyed and white-lipped to-morrow. I shan't be sorry, as, in that case, I can forbid her from attending the funeral."

"Do you mean Sandling's?"

"Yes. He is to be buried here. His son has cabled from Lucknow. It seems the married daughter in Kenya is too ill to be told what has happened. How are you? Pretty fit, I hope. Furneaux has just joined me for a whisky-and-soda. He wants to say something. . . Yes. I'll tell the young lady in the morning that you rang up."

In a few seconds came a high-pitched voice. "That you, Capitano? It's all in the news papers, I hear. I'm told they give a flattering but lifelike description of little me. The Chief will be green with envy. Don't be surprised, after this, if he takes to motor-cycling. Well, you and I may meet to-morrow. Where? Hasn't Sheldon wised you up? But you're going to dine with the Chief and him, so you'll be given full details. My own guess is that the Home Office is being consulted in the matter. And what do you think of the policeman's happy lot after a brief experience of it? It's a great life if you don't weaken. . . . Yes, I'm well aware that I'm doing all the talking. There are most convincing reasons why I can't let you butt in, because you want to ask questions, and I simply dare not answer. But the Chief, not having been here, will be full of information. If Pucci stages a capon, compliment your host on his carving, and he'll loosen up. By the way, do you know the American language? Yes? Well, see that you're well heeled before you get on the train. No, I didn't say 'oiled.' You're being flippant. Va t'en, donc! See you in the morning!"

And the connection was broken.

CHAPTER 12: THE PACK IN FULL CRY

WESTOBY was only too pleased to alter his own arrangements for the evening. By this time he was beginning to believe that the Yard had the situation well in hand, and that was a pleasant relief from the only-too-well-grounded forebodings of the past few days.

The two were on time at Pucci's, one of the few small and perfect Italian restaurants now left in a post-war London which hardly knows that such places exist, and will never realise what it has lost until their hospitable doors are closed for ever. The proprietor was a splendid advertisement of his wares, both food and wine. A short man, with tiny hands and feet, he measured sixty inches round his waist, so he resembled an animated top kept upright by centrifugal force. Evidently, any friends of Winter's were treated as distinguished visitors. Stout as he was, Pucci could move rapidly. Floating up a steep stairs like a small balloon, he ushered the newcomers into the presence with a fine bow, whereupon, seemingly as part of a time-honoured ritual, the Chief held up his right hand with thumb and fingers outstretched, and Pucci gurgled "Cinque!" to an attendant waiter.

There followed a pleasant discussion of the available menu, five cocktails were brought, Pucci drank one, and vanished.

Westoby was greatly interested.

"Does that fat man take a nip with each of his well-known customers?" he asked.

"No," said Winter. "I have reason to believe that he will not touch a drop of any kind of liquor till the next time some of the men from the Yard dine here, and our visits average one a week."

Westoby laughed.

"Sorry," he said, with disarming good humour. "This is new territory to me. My horizon has widened considerably during the past twenty-four hours."

The Chief smiled, too. He knew what good fellows Staff colonels could be when the slight frostiness induced by red or blue or green tabs disappears.

"Pucci is really an institution," he explained pleasantly. "He represents Soho at its best. You know Inspector Furneaux, Captain Mannering? I hope you will bring Colonel Westoby here some evening when Furneaux and Pucci are in good form. He will be amused. And now, I may as well say, walls have ears here as elsewhere. I suggest that we make no allusion whatever to the business which has brought us together until the table is cleared."

The hint was taken. Shooting, racing, the shortcomings of the Government—anything except crime, whether local or international, was discussed during the meal. At last Winter was free to throw light on the dark places of the Sandling murder. He had not uttered many words before the soldiers, who thought themselves fairly well acquainted with the ins and outs of a peculiar affair, grasped the essential fact that ever since the Criminal Investigation Department was informed that the great chemist had given his life for a fad, not Great Britain alone, but the whole of Western Europe had been scoured to discover not only who killed him, but why he had been killed.

"Of course, the history of Sir William's invention goes back to the 1917-18 period of the Great War, when every nation was trying to find the deadliest and most easily distributed gas," he said. "There can be no doubt that a curious experience which befell our friend Mannering as a boy put the idea of marsh gas as a semi-explosive, fatal both as a flame and a monoxide, into his old-time professor's mind. The end of the war did not stop scientific research in that direction. It has gone on ceaselessly all over the world, wherever there are chemists and laboratories. Somehow, probably by a careless word spoken in a moment of enthusiasm, Dr. Vorhinoff, a Russian, learnt of Sandling's discovery, or theory, as we may term it, since it must have been little more than a nebulous idea until quite recently. We know why he wanted to get hold of it—to destroy Bolshevism. The Bolsheviks themselves came next. They were eager to secure a weapon which would oust capitalism in the only effective way. The Germans were in the field soon afterwards, and their anxiety to penetrate Sandling's secret may or may not have been inspired by a desire for mere self-protection. However, here we have three well-defined foreign agencies, controlling ample funds and served by determined men and women, each opposed to the others, but all sworn to deprive Great Britain, the one nation which might be trusted in the matter, of the safeguarding of such a means of destruction, because our people would never sanction its use in an unprovoked attack. Let me put in an explanatory word here. Sir William's formula was tested fully this afternoon at Aldershot, and it proved a complete and rather pitiful failure."

At this point the Chief seemed to suspect that the outer leaf of his cigar was not burning smoothly, so he examined it carefully.

"Is that an official report to the War Office?" inquired Mannering, after a marked pause.

"Yes."

"Could any other sort of report be looked for?"

"Not unless the War Office employed a set of perfect idiots to conduct the experiments," growled Westoby.

Winter's cigar seemed to be on its good behaviour again. He blew out a large smoke-ring and darted several smaller ones through it.

"No one could have stated the essential features of that part of the inquiry more clearly than you two gentlemen," he purred blandly. "Well, as Captain Mannering is leaving for Edinburgh at eleven o'clock, I must defer any elaborate analysis of the tricks and wiles employed on Sir William by the emissaries of the Continental groups I have described, nor is it necessary now to deal with the immense difficulties imposed on nearly every Department of the British Government by the inventor's peculiar notions. I may say, briefly, that I believe he meant to retain the ultimate control in his own hands. He, and none other, should decide what was best and wisest in the interests of humanity. That was too large an order for any man, or number of men. That is, and must ever remain, the hidden purpose of the Power that created mankind and all pertaining thereto. His craze cost him his life. The stupid fools who ran him to earth, and, as we shall surely ascertain, gave him the alternative of selling his secret or being murdered forthwith, are obsessed, in their turn, with the notion that they alone are destined to be the arbiters of human progress. They are not. We know now who they are. We even know their names and where they are lodging to-night in Glasgow. Their present plan is escape to-morrow evening on a vessel sailing from Leith to the Baltic by way of Kristiansund and Stockholm. We could arrest them at once if we wished, but, owing to the restrictions of English law, to say nothing of Scottish procedure, we prefer to charge them straight away with the crime rather than grab them on suspicion.

"You, Captain Mannering, are the direct witness. The two ghouls whom you saw on Tuesday afternoon at Blackdown Farm killed Sir William and tried afterwards to dispose of his body. You alone can identify them beyond dispute. If you do so, the way of the law will be made clear. If you fail they will still be arrested, but their ultimate conviction will not be quite so speedy and certain. That is why you are going North to-night. You will meet Mr. Furneaux in Edinburgh to-morrow about noon. He will arrange matters with the authorities there and in Leith. I can say no more on this point. It would be manifestly unfair if I were to give you such indications as to the manner and present semblance of this pair of criminals that you could hardly fail to recognise them at sight. Do not misunderstand me. You would not wilfully draw an unfair inference, but we have to remember that they will be defended, and an adroit counsel would try and weaken your evidence if he could show that the police had described them before you see them to-morrow in conditions differing vastly from those which obtained when you first set eyes on them. You will find Furneaux scrupulously fair in this matter. He will not say: 'Are those the men you watched at the farm?' but rather: 'Have you ever seen those men before? If so, where, and what were they doing?' There is a vast distinction between the two questions."

"I would know one of the blighters if he were half cremated," said Mannering. "I could not sum up the other one so closely, but—well, I suppose I had better stop at that. May I ask if some of your very exact information is due to the attack on Miss Hardacre this morning?"

"Yes. A little French Communist grew quite talkative when Furneaux tackled him."

"I thought as much. But why in the world should that poor girl's life have been endangered in such a way?"

"Criminals who use automatic pistols and high-powered cars do not consult the police as to the nature or extent of their operations."

"Sorry, but I shall take some convincing that the North Riding police, if not Scotland Yard, did not slip a cog when they allowed Miss Hardacre to be kidnapped."

The Chief bridled somewhat under Mannering's steady stare. The truth was that he himself suspected a slight lack of foresight somewhere up in the North— Superintendent Dunkeld, for instance, might have been warned much earlier—but sheer esprit de corps prevented him from admitting it, and, indeed, he had not yet learnt the exact circumstances of the attack on Betty. "I might contend that they prevented it most effectually," he said stiffly.

"Yet none knows better than you that her rescue was largely accidental."

"Hold on a moment!" broke in Westoby. "Aren't you being a trifle unfair to the police, Mannering? It seems to me that this Foxton incident was arranged deliberately to throw dust in the eyes of the authorities. What better way of weakening pursuit elsewhere than by staging another outrage close to the scene of the first one?"

"May I put in a word?" said Sheldon quietly. "Girard, the Frenchman, told Furneaux that neither he nor any of the others in his party knew that Miss Hardacre had never met Sir William. The only definite information they had about her was given by a man working in the show ground. This fellow has been found and questioned and seems to be innocent of any active collusion. They hoped, however, that Miss Hardacre might have some knowledge of Sir William's work, and meant to frighten her into revealing it. That is all. She was not in any real peril."

"One fact is patent, at any rate—this young woman must be devilish good looking," growled Westoby.

That was quite the right word. Even Mannering laughed and decided to drop the argument.

He was making himself comfortable in a sleeping-car in King's Cross Station about 10.45 p.m. when a well-dressed, square youngster who was a total stranger tackled him, and, having made sure he was addressing Captain Mannering and none other, handed over a note. It was from the Chief, and read: "Miss Bingham contrived to leave the train before arriving at Harwich. She returned alone, went straight to Welbeck Street, called you on the phone, and, being assured that you had gone out, actually went to your club. She has made no attempt to communicate with Scotland by telegram or telephone. Of course, if she thinks fit, she will be permitted to do so, because she's a mischievous young person. Will you oblige me by telling the bearer whether, by any chance, let the hall-porter or any of the club servants know that you were bound for Scotland?"

"Who wrote this?" said Mannering, looking Winter's messenger straight in the face.

"The Chief, of course, sir," came the sur prised reply.

"Well, I want you to say I did not even tell my taxi-driver that I was making for King's Cross. He took me to Tottenham Court Road, and I changed cabs there. Sir William Sandling's butler helped me to pack about a quarter past seven. He could not help knowing I was preparing for a journey."

"Oh, that's all right, sir," smiled the young detective. "It was Wilkins who gave us the tip about Miss Bingham's return. Our chaps in Harwich were horribly upset. They pinched four men, but could not make out how they missed the woman."

When the train started Mannering began to write. He was determined that if exact knowledge of the present position of affairs in this extraordinary case would prove helpful, Betty should possess it. Being, as he admitted afterwards, "a child in such matters," he did not realise that his singular solicitude for her well being might convey quite a different impression from the record of political and almost dynastic complications which he meant her to have at her fingers' ends. Most certainly her woman's heart did not fail to interpret his anxiety aright. When a young man sets out to tell a young woman at great length how closely she is bound up with a most serious plot against the peace of the world, yet warns her in every paragraph that her own personal safety is the one essential thing in so far as he is concerned—well, she is apt to dwell more on remarks of that sort than on the considerations which would weigh with the Home Secretary.

He got the Pullman car attendant to post the letter at York, and it was in Betty's hands about the time he reached Edinburgh.

*   *   *   *   *

Furneaux and he were destined to undergo a trying ordeal at Leith after a somewhat dull morning spent in the Scottish capital. They could hardly indulge in sight-seeing, because they knew not the moment when the telephone might summon them. And, in the event, they found themselves in action rather unexpectedly. It was assumed that their quarry, having handed over the car to associates in Newcastle, would cross Scotland from Glasgow by train, but it was evidently thought advisable to minimise the risk of being seen en route, so the fugitives were rushed away from Clyde-side by fellow "Reds" in closed car.

The Scottish police were not to be headed of the trail in that easy way, however. Edinburgh was informed five minutes after they had started, and Furneaux took Mannering to Leith Dock fully an hour before the wanted men could possibly arrive there.

It was interesting to note that the detective: left nothing to chance at this final stage in the man-hunt.

"I have never understood," he said, while the two were skirting the Calton Hill in a taxi, "why the working classes in the large towns of Scotland should be so impregnated with Communism. Can you conceive any form of thought so utterly opposed to the accepted notions of Scottish mentality and characteristics? But there you are! As the late and not greatly lamented President Cleveland said once, 'It is a condition, not a theory,' and we have to allow for the fact that a set of rotten crooks and murderers can count on thousands of sympathisers in the hard-headed North simply because they are regarded as the fighting force of Bolshevism. So, even in Leith, their scouts will be posted. We must humbug them."

And the humbugging was done most neatly, though, of course in this, as in every other phase of life, the best-laid schemes may miscarry.

Mannering was handed over to the Chief of the Passport Office near the quay at which the steamer was moored. He was disposed of in such fashion that he could see all intending travellers quite clearly. A simple code of signals was arranged. The two men would hardly present themselves for examination at the same moment, so he was warned not to be worried if no one seemed to pay heed when he picked out the first one.

Obviously, a secret method of reporting "suspects" now in operation at many points of departure for the Continent cannot be revealed to-day in cold print. But it worked without a hitch In fact, it was so effective that the watcher grew uneasy when, after an hour and a half of unremitting vigilance, he had to confess that none who passed the barrier bore any resemblance to either of the wanted criminals, though, by this time, the steamer's siren had hooted a loud signal that the shore gangway was about to be disconnected.

Furneaux showed himself at last, and Mannering was positively grateful that the little man did not seem unduly perturbed.

"Nothing doing?" came the nonchalant question.

"Nothing. I am quite sure—"

"Of course you are! I hardly imagined that things would be made quite so easy as all that. As the old adage has it, 'There's many a slip 'twixt the cop and the ship.' However, being in Scotland, we must mak' siccar, and cover the whole ground. We just have time to take a peep at the pair who actually engaged the cabins, because they went on board fully half an hour ago. They will be at the purser's office by the time we get there, and any last minute arrivals will be detained until we reach the gangway again."

If nothing else, Furneaux succeeded in frightening the two nondescripts whom he found paraded for inspection. They were certainly not the murderous couple of Blackdown Farm, but it might have been quite safe to detain them "on suspicion," because the simplicity of their efforts to appear unconscious of any close scrutiny was almost amusing.

The detective asked for their passports, which were quite in order. Indeed, the British authorities are well aware that no sort of informality ever attaches itself to the "papers" of foreign rogues. But, in each instance, under the heading "Any special Peculiarities," was a descriptive entry.

One man, an alleged Finn, had "a white, cicatrised scar, on neck, extending from under the left ear to nearly the centre of the throat." Furneaux examined it closely, affected to refer to some memoranda in a notebook, and snapped a sudden question: "Why did you try to commit suicide, Anton?"

Mr. Bucovitch explained, in fluent French, that he was a cavalry soldier in the war, and his wound had been caused by a lance thrust.

The other was ready to show a machine-gun "pattern" on his right shoulder, but was excused.

"When did you two leave Glasgow?" demanded the detective.

Both men professed not to understand, so the query was repeated in French, whereupon Bucovitch was compelled to answer.

"We came here by car," he said.

"With whom?"

"Some friends who are employed in a chemical works on the Clyde."

"And where did you drop Luvitsky and Vereschagin?"

It was curious to note how swarthy skin can blanch and dark eyes grow lighter under the stress of sudden emotion. However, the travellers had been schooled to resist this attack. They vowed by false gods that they knew neither Luvitsky nor Vereschagin.

"Oh yes, you do!" cackled Furneaux, scowling at them. "Take my advice, and, when you get back to Moscow, stop there, which is more than Luvitsky or Vereschagin will ever have a chance of doing. You might also tell your friends in the Cheka that they would be better employed setting their own house in order than in putting forth vain efforts to crush England. You pair of stupid animals! Can't you see that you are being allowed to escape now because the British police refuse to bother about you? And, among other things, don't forget that you have been photographed at least six times during the past half-hour, so you will walk straight into prison if ever you dare show your noses again on this side of the North Sea."

The detective's obvious contempt, no less than the torrent of idiomatic French he poured forth, seemed to cow Bucovitch and his companion more than the suspicion that they might be concerned in a crime. They did not attempt to defend themselves. Indeed, as the purser reported afterwards, they were profoundly relieved when Furneaux turned on his heel, though he took occasion to search their baggage before they were permitted to go to their cabin.

No last-minute passengers boarded the ship before her steel hawsers were cast loose and she started on her voyage. A telephonic inquiry had been made already by Leith from Glasgow, and Glasgow was not only sure that the wanted men had gone west in a certain car, but undertook to grab the said car and its occupants when the return journey was made.

"A fat lot of good that will do!" sighed Furneaux when a disappointed police inspector informed him of Glasgow's excellent intentions.

"Weel, it may help a bit," protested the Scot vexedly. "What I can't mak' oot is why you didna have these fellows collared last necht when it was known whaur they were hidden."

"That was my original suggestion "—and Mannering marvelled at his friend's meek tone—"but the Home Office turned it down, on the plea that in this case proper identification should precede and not follow arrest. However, don't worry, inspector! We'll get them all right!"

"I'm no sae sure."

"Bet you a new hat we have them under lock and key within forty-eight hours!"

"I have no parteecular use for a new hat."

"So it's a foregone conclusion that you would win. All right! Let it go at that!"

But what will you dae noo, Maister Furneaux?"

"Take a taxi back to Edinburgh. I would sweat blood if I had to remain in Leith another five minutes!"

Mannering, of course, kept clear of this discussion. He was inclined to sympathise with the local policeman, who naturally wanted to be associated with the capture of two such eminent malefactors as the murderers of Sir William Sandling. However, the inspector seemed to be quite satisfied because he had forced Furneaux into a display of temper.

"Ay, ay!" he agreed. "Leith's a bonnie toon, but it's no fitted for the likes o' you."

At that moment a taxi drew up at the entrance to the dock, and a young man alighted. The first glimpse of him evoked some memory in Mannering's brain, but it was too elusive to convey enlightenment. The new arrival gazed around eagerly, and seemed to be almost elated when he set eyes on Mannering and Furneaux.

He hurried towards them with a curious certainty of manner.

"Captain Mannering?" he said. And Detective-Inspector Furneaux?"

"It would be a pity, Mr. Hardacre, if the introductions were not complete," said Furneaux. "Let me present you to Inspector Macgregor, of the Leith Constabulary."

The youngster seemed rather taken aback, but, being full of his errand, did not hesitate.

"I can't guess why any of you gentlemen should know my name," he said, "but that does not matter at the moment. My sister Betty arrived in Newcastle to-day shortly before ten o'clock. She had wired me beforehand, so I met her at the station, and came on with her to Edinburgh, having obtained a day's leave from my firm. But, look here, we are losing valuable time! Hop into this taxi. While we're driving to the Waverley Hotel I'll tell you what's going on."

"Anything to do with the two men we are after?"

"Everything. Betty has seen them, and she is trying to keep in touch."

"Come along, inspector!" yelped Furneaux. "It's only fair that you should bear a hand."

Hardacre, a well-set-up youngster eighteen months younger than his sister, and already a trusted subordinate in one of the great engineering works on Tyneside, recited an amazing story in a straightforward way, though he had the diffident air of one who expected at any moment to be ridiculed for talking nonsense. Betty, it appeared, had motored to Stockton soon after receiving Mannering's letter. She left her car there, but brought Tags, and the two caught a fast train to Newcastle. Between that city and Edinburgh she had plenty of time to acquaint her brother with the complexities of the Sandling case. He, of course, had read of her sensational escape the previous day and had telegraphed for assurance of her well-being, but he little imagined that she was so closely bound up in the major tragedy.

I couldn't understand just why we were rushing to Edinburgh," he explained, "but she said she was impelled to make the journey by something you said, Mr. Furneaux."

For once, the enfant terrible of Scotland Yard was nonplussed.

"Something I said!" he repeated. "She hadn't the remotest notion yesterday evening that I would be in Scotland to-day. The local superintendent of police was the only man in Yorkshire who knew where I was going, and I shall be very surprised if he – "

"That's all right," put in Mannering quietly. "I wrote the whole story while coming North last night, and got the letter 'expressed' from York. Miss Hardacre would receive it about eight o'clock this morning."

"She did," said brother Frank. "I read it!" Being a sharp-eyed young man, he noticed that Furneaux gave Mannering what he described later as "a look of hate," but its recipient smiled blandly.

"I hope I've said nothing wrong," he went on. "I only want to put you gentlemen in possession of the actual facts."

"Carry on!" said Furneaux, grinning vindictively. "Have you, by any chance, posted 'the whole story' back to some girl in Newcastle?"

"I?" cried Hardacre. "I wouldn't dream of doing such a thing!"

"When a suitable opportunity offers, take Mr. Mannering on one side and give him at great length your reasons for such admirable self-repression. . . . Well, what happened when you two reached Edinburgh?"

"Betty described Mr. Mannering and you to the hall-porter at the hotel, and he said you had taken a taxi down the Leith Road about two hours earlier. We were just about to come after you when a private car drew up a few yards short of the hotel entrance. A short, stiffly-built little fellow got out and hurried in the direction of the Waverley Station. He carried himself in a rather peculiar way, with a sort of dancing step, and his right shoulder was higher than his left. Betty seemed to be greatly interested, and was going to say something when the car stopped a second time, some fifty yards farther on, and a tall fellow appeared. He, too, made for the station, so he had to pass us, and I had a good look at him. By Jove! I've not often seen a nastier piece of work than his face, and we get some queer specimens in Newcastle from all parts of the world. Betty did not seem to gaze at him at all, but grabbed Tags and slung him into the depths of the hall-porter's office. No sooner was this second customer clear of the door, however, than she whispered in my ear: 'Frankie, those are the wanted men! I'm sure of it! Ask the hall-porter to take care of Tags—he might give me away, and I daren't risk it—then drive like mad to Leith

Dock and find Mr. Mannering and Mr. Furneaux. If they have made no arrest, bring them back here, and I'll contrive, somehow or other, to leave a note saying what is happening.' Naturally, I wanted to argue, but she simply wouldn't listen, so I did the next best thing—obeyed orders.

"All that's left for any of us to do," said Furneaux grimly. "This is the day of the super woman. There is no limit to her achievements. She can dance all night, lash at a golf ball all day, and fly the Atlantic or fall into it or swim it next morning—it's all the same to her—but I never thought she'd put one over on Scotland Yard—in the cause of law and order, I mean. On the other side, she's our most subtle enemy. Well, well! Here we are in Auld Reekie once more As Mr. Mannering wrote full details to Miss Hardacre, let's hear what Miss Hardacre has written to Mr. Mannering!"

CHAPTER 13: THE CHASE HEADS FOR THE SOUTH

BETTY was as good as her word. A railway porter had brought a note to the hotel. It was addressed: "Mr. Mannering, Mr. Furneaux, or Mr. Hardacre," and it ran: "The big man has booked for London. I have not seen the other one yet, so I assume he is already in the train, which starts at 1.50. The guard says we stop at Newcastle, Darlington, and York. May I suggest that Superintendent Dunkeld should meet me at York, as I am a stranger to the police in the other towns? By that time, too, I shall know exactly where to locate both men. If all goes well, I shall get off at York and return to Foxton, so someone may be able to bring Tags there. Mr. Furneaux will understand why I followed the trail to Edinburgh. I am simply putting into practice his theory of static electricity.

"B.

"P.S .—Of course, I may be altogether mistaken, but my fellow-travellers certainly fit into the picture conveyed by Mr. Mannering. Per haps Mr. Furneaux can give Mr. Dunkeld a lot more details by this time. Frankie will describe men.—B.

"P.P.S.—I'll send telegrams to York from Newcastle and Darlington .—B."

The detective's spasm of annoyance seemed to vanish while he listened to this remarkable document, which was handed to Frank Hardacre in the first instance, only to be passed on by him to Mannering. The latter did not hesitate to read it. He was determined that no move affecting Betty's safety should be made without his cognisance, and he did the C.I.D. the grave injustice of suspecting that Furneaux would not hesitate to imperil Betty or anybody else rather than allow the criminals to escape.

For all that, he was not misled by a certain deceptive quality of meekness in the little man's attitude.

"Very well put!" was Furneaux's prompt tribute. "Not many men living, and none of my acquaintance in the Yard, could have set forth the facts more clearly in a couple of minutes and in the midst of all the noise and bustle of departure of a main-line express. Do you recommend that I should get Superintendent Dunkeld on the phone without further delay, Captain Mannering?"

This silky inquiry produced a good-humoured retort. "As a preliminary, perhaps, you might stop pulling my leg!"

"A most unkind remark! How have I earned it? Haven't I thrust you into the limelight for days on end?"

Hardacre, of course, imagined that the two were on the verge of a quarrel.

"Oh, I say!" he bleated. "You shouldn't feel hipped about anything Betty has done. Dash it all! It was sheer luck that brought her and me to the entrance of this hotel at the very moment the car pulled up and some of the crowd inside behaved so curiously."

At that instant Tags barked, saying as plainly as possible: "What have I done that I should be shut up in here and closed out of all the fun?"

Mannering and Furneaux laughed. Hardacre looked puzzled, as well he might. The Leith inspector, who kept a still tongue, was more convinced than ever that the representative of Scotland Yard was light-headed. In fact, at the moment, he was reviewing the very definite instructions he had received that morning, because he wanted to make quite sure he had not been befooled by some practical joker, or worse.

"Oh, very well!" sighed the detective. "It's a nice state of affairs when the fly cop of the Yard has to be spurred into action by the voice of a valiant pup. . . . Mr.

Hardacre, will you kindly rescue Tags? If he hasn't a lead, we must get one, because Mr. Mannering is indicated for the pleasant task of restoring him to his mistress at Foxton to-morrow. Then we'll all pile into our taxi and go to police headquarters."

"You can phone from the hotel," broke in Inspector Macgregor. Not only did he want to hear of something definite being done, but he was by no means anxious that the chase should be handed over to his Edinburgh colleagues.

"I think it will take a weight off your mind if you see that I am received with open arms in Parliament Square," said Furneaux sweetly. "But that is a mere quip. A much better reason is that we are less liable to be bothered by listeners-in if we use an official phone. In any case, it is our natural centre. Let us establish connection there, and then return here for a solid meal."

"How about an aeroplane?" said Mannering.

"Nothing doing. I doubt if such a thing is immediately available north of the Tweed. When your true Scot gangs Sooth he takes a perfectly reliable train and pays third-class single fare. Isn't that so, inspector?"

"Weel," was the cautious answer, "I ken fine what I wad dae!"

Tags was brought into the party, and Mannering saw to it that the hall-porter was fully instructed and tipped reasonably. When en route Furneaux explained that, no matter how many planes they had at command, Mannering ought not to take any part in the prospective arrests at York.

"Your job is to pick out these rascals unaided," he said. "Certainly you might contrive to do that in the train, but an adroit counsel would discredit your evidence, since you would be compelled to admit that Miss Hardacre, who has never seen either man before to-day—her glimpse of one of them at six hundred yards can hardly count—had indicated to you where they would probably be found. No. You come on the screen, I hope, at an identification parade early to-morrow in York, when the conditions will be essentially the same as in the shed where the boat passengers gathered at Leith Dock within the past two hours. Am I recht, inspector?"

"Ay, ye're recht," admitted Macgregor grimly.

He was quite certain there was a screw loose somewhere, so the reaction was all the greater when a high official at Police Chambers hurried forward the instant Furneaux's name was announced, and, looking in surprise at Mannering and Hardacre, cried eagerly: "Have you got 'em?"

It was a trying moment for the two younger men, but Furneaux was magnanimous.

"No," he said instantly. "They took fright and left the car en route. In fact, they are now well on the way to London. Take us to your private phone, and ask the trunk line to give every possible facility for a couple of long-distance calls, one to Foxton in Yorkshire, and the other to the Yard. Then you will hear the whole sad story."

"Do you mean that the wanted men are on the 1.50?"

"Yes."

"But why waste time? We can have the train stopped and searched within the next twenty minutes."

"How true! We can sacrifice several lives, and give a pair of well-armed and desperate criminals a very reasonable chance of making a successful getaway. . . . No. York is our best bet. You will know why when I get in touch with Superintendent Dunkeld, whom I have warned to stand fast until I tell him what has happened here."

The Edinburgh man was silenced, though not convinced. However, the Scottish authorities had been asked to assist Furneaux rather than take direct action, so he waived the point. Like Inspector Macgregor, he was glad of his own reticence before the detective had finished with Dunkeld and began repeating his information to an attentive Chief in the big offices on the Embankment. To ease the situation all round, Furneaux affected to explain to Winter why York was the only practicable place where the arrests could be made in comparative safety.

"Of course," he said, "we could grab them at Newcastle or Darlington, but, as Miss Hardacre's alert intelligence warned her, she would have to make herself known to the police, and one can hardly expect men not well posted in the details to tackle Luvitsky and Vereschagin with the instant decisiveness Dunkeld and his merry lads will show. There may be shooting, of course. If so, the Yorkshire police will try and shoot first, a simple faith which the Norman bloods in the other towns could not possibly display. As for, halting the train at a wayside station, it is not to be thought of. The moment it pulled up the enemy would be on the alert. I trust Dunkeld to the limit. If anything goes wrong it will not be his fault. For instance, he thought at first of getting on the train at Darlington, for which he has plenty of time, but that would mean a search for Miss Hardacre, and taking her by surprise, perhaps in the very compartment where one or both of the Boishies may be seated. But that marvellous young woman has risked her life often enough already. From now on she must be safeguarded. . . . Eh, what's that? I'm not making a speech. Those few kind words are intended for other ears than yours. During the past half-hour Captain Mannering has been more than anxious to treat me with brutal violence, while an inspector from Leith, a splendid fellow, doubts every statement I make. You see, the blighters blame me because the foxes have doubled."

He hung up the receiver dejectedly, and seemed not to notice the sympathetic grins evoked by that concluding comment.

"And what do you propose doing now, Mr. Furneaux?" inquired the local official.

"We're going back to the hotel to eat. Won't you come with us? You'll hear a great yarn and be all the more keyed up for the denouement, which should get through

about seven o'clock. Then we four can leave Caledonia
stern and wild at 10.50."

By this time the North had grown wary.

"You are including the dog, I suppose?" came the
guarded question.

"That's one way of putting it. The fact is that Tags has
included himself in every act since the bronzed hero from
India and the charming lecturer on technology met on a
Yorkshire moor last Tuesday afternoon. But why spoil a
thrilling story? Shall we walk? Perhaps Tags may catch a
haggis on the way. He has really earned some slight
relaxation of the sort."

Young Hardacre elected to keep Mannering company.

"Is it really true," he said, when free to speak without
being overheard, "that my sister and you met for the first
time on Tuesday?"

"Yes, it's true enough, though I can hardly believe it
myself. Why do you ask?"

Well, Betty had so much to say about you. She's not
one of the gushing sort, you know. I've never —Well, I
was sure you were old friends, and knew each other in
Leeds, or somewhere. And, then—while coming here this
morning, she showed me your letter."

The boy hesitated. He hardly knew what to say, and
he certainly missed the quite definite blush which
changed Mannering's complexion from "bronze" to a
brick-red for a few seconds

"Naturally you are puzzled," came the slow admission.
"Of course, you hardly realise yet how much your sister
has endured since I halted her on the road near
Blackdown Farm. She and I seem to have lived through
as many months as there have been days in the interim.
Unhappily, her ordeal has not ended yet. I shall not have
a moment's peace until I hear she is safe and sound in Dr.
Lysaght's house, or wherever else she may be going after
leaving York."

"Oh, don't you worry!" cried confident youth. "Betty
can look after herself all right. She was taken by surprise

yesterday morning. Those bounders in the car didn't give her half a chance. But this time she's ready for a row. Why, when she was fifteen and my brother Jack and I were two and three years younger, she could put it all over us with the gloves."

Betty herself might not have been altogether pleased had she overheard this glowing account of her bygone prowess in the "noble art." By this time, however, she was trying to visualise the situation which would probably confront her at York four hours later.

She had located her quarry quickly enough. The tall man, Luvitsky, as it happened, and his confederate, Vereschagin (an Odessa Jew masquerading under a well-known Russian name), were separated by the whole length of the train. From this fact she argued that they would remain apart during the journey, no matter where it ended, and she knew already that Luvitsky had bought a ticket for London. For some reason—probably owing to Mannering's version of events at the farm—she regarded this man as the master villain of the pair, so she determined to keep a close watch on him at each stopping-place. He made no move, however, at either Newcastle or Darlington.

From the first of these towns Betty telegraphed to the Chief Constable at York the exact positions of the coaches, the numbers of the seats occupied by both men, and her own chosen place in the corridor of the leading coach. From Darlington she wired "No change," but that message could hardly have affected the ultimate outcome, because the authorities had provided against every foreseen contingency before it reached Dunkeld on the platform. Ultimately, events took their own course. They always do, as every man knows who has ever been engaged in a life-and-death grapple with the denizens of the underworld, and especially with that fanatical section of it which gratifies its criminal instincts by pleading political necessity.

Oddly enough, the one uncertain factor in a drama now fast speeding to its final curtain was that which no one, least of all Betty herself, took into account. How long could any normally constituted young woman withstand the fierce strain of existence in the conditions which had obtained since she was first brought into such close and unceasing contact with the murder of Sir William Sandling? Not for a minute had the tension been really relaxed. The two days at the farm, the terribly easy way in which she had almost been carried off by a pack of human wolves, the strong dose of bromide which alone had induced sleep after that most trying experience, and now the long hours in throbbing car and fast-rushing express trains, culminating in the protracted vigil of the journey from Edinburgh to York—these things must have a cumulative effect—it was only a question of time before even an exceptionally healthy body and well-balanced mind would yield and cry for rest.

As might be expected, the crisis came at the worst possible moment. The train was slowing up as it swept past the first curve of the half-mile-long main-line platform at York when Betty yielded to an unreasonable and almost frenzied panic. She was sure that everything would go wrong. After firmly resisting the temptation to seek even the passive aid of a ticket collector she was convinced now that she ought to have had the suspected men watched by cohorts of dining-room stewards and other train officials when York was neared. The hurrying crowds in the station itself were affrighting. How could she pick out Superintendent Dunkeld among the hundreds of moving people and the scores of uniformed employees? Her eyes swam and there was a loud buzzing in her ears. She could see nothing, hear nothing. Everything was a blur. She supposed one felt that way before collapsing in a faint. Then a surge of anger, amounting almost to frenzy, helped her more than a little. Why, if she gave in like this she would simply drop into the superintendent's arms, supposing she ever found him, and crumple up in the silliest way.

So she leaned out through the lowered window of the door near which she .had stationed herself, when, lo and behold! there stood Mr. Dunkeld, but in plain clothes, smiling up at her. And, quite miraculously it seemed, be said exactly the right thing.

"Here we are!" he exclaimed cheerfully. "Follow the platform inspector along the corridor, glance into the fourth compartment, see if our Russian friend is still in the window seat with his back to the engine, and, if so, nod to me. I shall be just behind you. Don't wait a second, but go ahead. The inspector will let you out at the other end of the carriage and take you to the rear coach, where you can indicate the whereabouts of Russki No. 2 to a man who will be waiting there. Now, mind you, on no account do you halt anywhere. Stick to the inspector. He will look after you."

Betty was recovering rapidly, but she certainly failed to notice that the platform inspector had to unlock the door before either he or Dunkeld could enter. Nor was she aware that a number of surprised passengers, who could not get out through that or any other door, were also being shouldered out of the way rather unceremoniously by the said inspector. As a matter of fact, the superintendent had little enough time at his disposal to say all that was absolutely necessary. He could not possibly explain that as the outcome of instructions sent to Darlington, every door in the front and rear coaches was locked before the train reached York, and no passenger would be allowed to leave or enter those sections of the train until a man deputed for the purpose gave the "All clear" signal.

The girl made no mistake in identifying Luvitsky, who, as a fellow-traveller testified afterwards, had hardly moved since his departure from Edinburgh. He neither read a newspaper or book, nor smoked. He tried to sleep, but made rather a failure of the effort, so, for the most part, he gazed out on the passing landscape on his side of the carriage, and thus, as it happened, missed nearly every object of interest en route. He was quick-witted enough, however, to realise now that some slight but unusual commotion had arisen in the corridor. It chanced that none of the other three men in the compartment was getting out at York, so when the door opened and Dunkeld entered, followed closely by a pair of heavily built youngsters, who looked as though they could tackle and hold a bull between them, he was given a bare second's warning that the avengers were on him.

Still, the superintendent himself was a most mild-mannered man in appearances so Luvitsky's instant decision was amazingly swift and confident. By chance, as it seemed then, he was engaged already in lowering the window of the outer door. Now he dived through it head first, catching the external handle with his right hand, and thrusting his feet so violently against Dunkeld's body that good fortune alone saved the latter from grave, if not fatal, injuries. As it was, the Bolshevik agent won clear, and swung himself round, awkwardly it is true, but with sufficient physical control that he was able to drop on all fours on the six-foot way.

Then he must have felt himself tackled relentlessly, because his right hand went to a breast pocket, and the fierce snarl of an automatic announced the tearing away of his heart and some part of his lungs.

To all intents and purposes, Dunkeld was in the time-honoured position of the engineer hoist by his own petard. That door, its use being prohibited, had to be locked in any case. He sank breathlessly into the very seat vacated by the Russian, and gasped feebly, though with a smile: "It's all right, gentlemen—the blighter has shot himself—good riddance!"

He did not add that Luvitsky had simply fallen from the frying-pan into the fire. Fully half a dozen policemen were gathered on the line at the exact place where each marked coach would halt, while others patrolled every yard of the opposite platform. The station-master had arranged that no train would stand on or traverse any of the intervening rails until the south-bound express had been searched, so Luvitsky's spectacular attempt to escape on the blind side of the carriage could end only in utter failure.

"Still, it was a fine effort," Dunkeld admitted to Furneaux when the two met. "As a gymnastic trick evolved on the spur of the moment, it reminded me of the action of a cat rather than a man. I had it in my heart to be sorry for the poor fool. Even as he lost his balance he probably saw the blue-coated squad beneath. Then he knew!"

Not another soul in the compartment, or even in the whole carriage, was aware of the actual tragedy until the superintendent spoke. Hardly anyone on the departure platform gave any heed to the pistol-shot. Several free-born Britons were testifying loudly to the crass negligence of a railway company which locked doors and refused to open them, while a select few who had seen Betty whisked away by the inspector grew almost incoherent with wrath. Things were different, however, at the rear of the train. By this time pandemonium reigned there.

At first it was impossible to find out what was happening. Dunkeld, the one man who could have discerned the true sequence of events, was sick with pain and not able to move for many minutes. But, in the long run, the general trend of testimony showed that, in all likelihood, Luvitsky had told his fellow-fugitive to lean out through the window on the off side at York, and they could indicate to each other that all had gone well thus far. Undoubtedly Vereschagin had obeyed, so he was not only made aware of the policeman waiting beneath, but may have seen Luvitsky's dramatic departure from a thoroughly implacable world. Be that as it may, he banged up the window and almost leaped into the corridor, taking care, however, to skip nimbly over the feet of a lady and her husband who shared the compartment with him.

An athletic constable sprang up at the door, but could not open the window. The woman passenger saw him and interpreted his gesticulations correctly.

"John," she cried excitedly, "that man who has just gone is wanted by the police! Don't you think you ought to try and find out which way he is going?"

John was by no means anxious for the job. He had formed a most unfavourable opinion of Vereschagin the moment the latter entered the compartment at Edinburgh. For the rest of his days, however, he thanked his stars that he did not hesitate, and, indeed, many a man has been decorated for valour for incurring far less risk. He was in the corridor before his wife could lower the window, thus allowing the policeman to climb through.

Obviously, the representative of the law could not be sure that the evil-looking fellow who had vanished so suddenly was the person he sought, though such behaviour was suspicious and the description tallied. Vereschagin himself, however, resolved all doubt in the matter. Finding that he was caught like a rat in a trap, and unable even to reach the next coach—seeing a rush of ominously determined faces along the platform, and knowing that the ordinary avenues of escape were cut off—he, too, made a bold bid for the unexpected.

A railway official, yielding to the insistent demand of a York police-sergeant, unlocked a door. The Russian darted for it, firing over his shoulder at the constable now in pursuit, but luckily missing both him and "John." The shot, however, did secure a precious fraction of a second of delay, and two more bullets sent three men reeling from the exit. Then the sturdy ruffian leaped on to the window-sash, caught the top of the door with both hands, gained the roo: of the carriage, and ran forward quite rapidly and with some sort of set purpose.

P.C. Paxton, however, now took the stage. It was he to whom the platform inspector was leading Betty, but the two were nearly a hundred yards distant, and finding a good deal of difficulty in dodging hurrying passengers and hand-trucks laden with luggage. Paxton, of course, had a good view of the runner who chose such an unusual track and heralded his appearance by shooting his path clear. Moreover, the policeman had memorised the description supplied by both Betty and her brother. Without the least hesitancy, therefore, he whipped out a pistol and fired.

It was not such a difficult shot as it seemed, because bullet and target were moving on converging lines, so Paxton brought his man down with a broken thigh, and a steel rail did the rest when Vereschagin plunged headlong on to the permanent way.

Betty heard the shooting, saw the Russian lurch and fall, and recognised Paxton. After that she knew nothing whatsoever until she heard Dr. Lysaght say: "That's first-rate, Betty! Now, just another sip or two, and you'll be able to walk to my car. Bless your brave heart, there will be plenty of colour in your face before we're even clear of the city walls. . . . Dunkeld? Oh, he's all right, but he must remain here for the night. No. No one is badly hurt except the two star artists, of whom one is dead and the other dying. . . . Great Scott, where's that dog of yours? Not lost in the shuffle, I hope? Good! By the way, Dunkeld asked me to tell you he will soon be in touch with Edinburgh, so the worst is over, and everybody should be happy!"

CHAPTER 14: WHEREIN THE STORM BLOWS ITSELF OUT

THE London and North-Eastern station at York is not only a terminal point for many lines of traffic, but it bestrides a great artery of communication between the North and South of Great Britain. Never wholly restful during any hour of the twenty-four, it boils into a fury of human activity when an express from Edinburgh or London draws up at one of the central plat forms. Torrents of passengers and mounds of luggage converge on or flow from that particular train in every direction. The placid cathedral city itself contributes little to this sudden maelstrom. People gather there and disperse irrespective of the community which has been established on the banks of the Ouse since a period regarded even by Caesar's legions as prehistoric.

It follows, therefore, that travellers from all parts of England that day saw one or other of the Russians sent to his final account, while a select few, using the spacious gangway which spans the centre rails, witnessed both events.

Some of these onlookers counted themselves lucky. Others, again, gave way to panic; several women fainted, and quite a number of men, especially those who were fat and scant o' breath, ran like rabbits and suffered various contusions from falling down stairs. They were hardly to be blamed, because Paxton's bullet, had it missed the Russian, would probably have bagged some full-blooded Yorkshireman on the footbridge.

Hence there was frantic disorder during many minutes, and it could hardly be imagined that any member of the general public would be able to guess what had actually happened. Yet a smartly dressed and good-looking young woman, though nearly swept off her feet in the turmoil, did apparently succeed in doing that very thing.

It was evident that she meant to travel on the train from which all the excitement emanated. Her only encumbrance being a small handbag, she hurried to secure a seat, her clear intent being to board the leading passenger coach. This, of course, she was unable to do, but she happened to notice the peculiar way in which an officer of police and two constables were admitted to the carriage by a railway employee, while all others were barred from either getting in or out. She watched, too, the giving, by the leader of the small party, of an evidently confidential message to a very pretty though somewhat anxious-faced girl who seemed to be on the lookout for him. True, the police were not in uniform, but some clever folk, well versed in the ways of the world, can always dispense with labels of that sort.

Then she discerned dimly through two thicknesses of glass a scurry inside a compartment. Almost at the same instant the platform inspector helped Betty to alight, and locked the door again, disregarding the protests of other passengers who tried to follow. Meanwhile, this observant onlooker heard a pistol-shot, which came from some point practically underneath the carriage.

Having absorbed these details with really remarkable accuracy, it was not altogether sur prising that such a sharp-eyed observer should take an even more definite interest in Betty, and try to ascertain what became of her. Hence, she could not help watching Vereschagin's spectacular flight and its end.

Then, of course, the flood of humanity boiled into a sort of frenzy; yet, oddly enough, in view of her attitude thus far, the one person who had been vouchsafed more than a glimmering of the truth either lost her nerve, or determined to attend strictly to her own affairs. She stopped short at once, glanced at the train, and made for one of the many available carriages where some blithely unconscious travellers bound for the South were already taking their seats.

Hitherto she had shown a quite unfeminine coolness and self-possession in the midst of an uproar of which she alone among the hundreds surrounding her had measured the grave significance. Yet she literally quailed when she felt her right arm, which was free, the bag being in her left hand, grasped firmly above the elbow, while a man's voice said: "I'm sorry, Miss Bingham, but you cannot be allowed to return to London at present!"

The colour fled from her cheeks and lips, and her blue eyes flickered to a whitish grey. She was too frightened even to scream. She knew well that authority lay behind those quiet words, and it is probable that an ugly vista of alarming consequences opened up in the secret places of her brain with a speed not to be assessed by any scale of photographic exactness.

But she recovered her poise to some extent when she looked into the face of her captor. His expression was inscrutable, though not unfriendly, and she had never before seen him, to her know ledge. He was young, well dressed, and so different from the hectoring, bull-terrier type of Prussian policeman with which alone she was acquainted, that she grew unafraid.

"Who are you?" she demanded angrily. "What do you want? Let go my arm!"

She had to speak in that jerky way because her mind absolutely refused to frame longer or more emphatic sentences. She did, however, try to wrench herself free, whereupon the grip tightened remorselessly and was supplanted by a hand on her wrist.

"It is stupid to make a scene here," came the stern counsel. "I am a detective-inspector from Scotland Yard, and I have kept you under observation all day, ever since you received that telephone message from Glasgow this morning in Welbeck Street. I addressed you as Miss Bingham so as not to alarm you, but, if you compel me to it, I may treat you as Bertha von Buren, which will be a different matter altogether."

Then she literally wilted, and Sheldon knew that all the fight had gone out of her.

"I have done nothing wrong," she murmured. "I am not connected with those men. They are my enemies as much as yours. But I don't want to die, and my life would not have been safe in any part of the world if I had refused to help them to-day."

Truly a remarkable outburst! Sheldon felt bound to take advantage of it.

"Possibly—but how could you have helped?" he said.

"I don't know. Perhaps they wanted some assistance or direction when they reached. London. At any rate, I did not dare back out when asked to meet them at York on this train."

"Nothing was said about that when Grunbaum telephoned from Glasgow, yet you knew whom to look for!"

"Why not? Perhaps I knew better than you. Don't you realise, you thick-headed Englishman, that they are a menace to all the world, and that Germany is the first real barrier they have to break down!"

"Well, well! Allies, are we? I hope so. Now, give me your bag. I shall continue to hold your arm. Come with me quietly, and none will be the wiser."

"Where are you taking me to?"

"The station-master's office—in the first place."

"But why am I arrested? It comes to that, I suppose?"

"Because you only escaped arrest last night by doubling back from Harwich. Won't that answer suffice for the time being?"

"Ach, wass!" she muttered, with bitter disregard of pretence.

Mannering had been astonished by her candour during the luncheon at the Ritz, and Sheldon was equally surprised now. Perhaps she did not realise it, but this dropping of the cloak of British nationality was the best card she could possibly play.

They had cleared the crowd on the central plat forms, and were in front of a large bookstall which faces the main exit and booking-hall, when Dr. Lysaght and Betty's appointed guide, the railway inspector, appeared. Between them they were supporting, indeed, nearly carrying, a young woman who was quite evidently unaware of her actual surroundings.

"There she is!" announced Miss Bingham with singular vivacity. "That's the girl! She came in the train from Edinburgh and told, the police where they would find Luvitsky. They were waiting for her. She must be the Betty Hardacre whose name is in all the papers."

"You certainly are the limit," smiled Sheldon. "Now, listen to me. No one here knows who you are. Keep a still tongue in your head till I ask you to speak. I'll treat you quite fairly, so do as I tell you."

She nodded in a curiously offhand way, and watched Betty being led through a ticket barrier. That was how the two women met and parted, though the course of their lives had clashed in a most amazing way.

"She looks as though she has had a bad time," was the German girl's comment. "Well, it's a bit of a strain for any woman to be kidnapped and shot at. Perhaps, Mr. Policeman, you will understand now why I thought it safest to obey orders."

"Whose orders? The Cheka's?" said Sheldon instantly.

"Indirectly, yes; though Grünbaum, as you seem to know, is a German, and honest enough in his way—like me, you may be inclined to admit."

Sheldon did not attempt to answer. This variety of the feminine complex was new to him. Moreover, he had to usher Miss Bingham through double doors without attracting attention, and he was not quite sure yet that she would not make a foolish effort to escape.

She read his thought and smiled acidly, but uttered no word, because Sheldon was explaining to a puzzled clerk that he and the lady meant waiting there a few minutes until someone in authority came in from the platform. The youngster raised no difficulty. He knew already that things far removed from ordinary departmental routine were going on in York just then, and regarded the presence of this pretty, rather defiant-looking girl as a first instalment of the expected drama.

But several minutes passed and nothing happened.

Sheldon, of course, could not guess that Superintendent Dunkeld had been put out of action temporarily, and was then sitting on a barrow, hardly able to move, but forcing himself to give instructions to some of his own men and the railway people as to the safeguarding of the two bodies and a painstaking search for any luggage they might have brought with them in carriage or van. The latter, if any, he hardly expected to recover until the train reached King's Cross, but suitcases in the two compartments could be identified by what logicians term a process of exhaustion. As for the railway executive, every available man was engaged in restoring order and getting the train away on time.

At last Sheldon bethought him of telephoning to police headquarters in the city. He was on the point of putting through a call when a slightly built, middle-aged man, escorted by a constable in uniform, limped in, and, disregarding the counter-clerk, said: "Inspector Sheldon?"

"Yes," came the reply.

"My name is Dunkeld. I am sorry for the delay. One of those rascals winded me rather badly. I got Mr. Winter's message and meant coming along at once, because it was arranged that the prisoners should be brought here. But, as usual, the unexpected happened. . . . This the lady?"

"Yes."

"Well, suppose we get into my car and go to the City police station? It is no great distance. Want any help?"

"No," smiled Sheldon. "I have met with no difficulties of any sort, unless it was in minding my own job when the other affair started. I hope you are not badly hurt?"

"I think not. I seem to have missed any real injury. Thank goodness the blighter was not wearing hob-nailed boots!"

In the car, a five-seater tourer, the self-possessed Bertha was sandwiched between the two police officers, while the constable rode in front with the driver. They were hardly clear of the station approach before the girl spoke, and her ultra-English accent showed that her own dangerous predicament was not troubling her at all.

"You people may be making the mistake of your lives," she said calmly. "You have got rid of Luvitsky and Vereschagin —supposing they were the men who killed Sir William—but how do you know that they have not handed over the formula to others? Why, at this very moment it may be passing through your own post-office, en route to half a dozen different agencies before it reaches Russia."

Dunkeld was not to be blamed if he deemed this ingenuous prattler a typical poseur, but Sheldon was beginning to take her seriously, and, in the conditions, thought he knew how to handle her.

"Your solicitude on behalf of the British Government is quite touching," he said; "so you will be more than relieved to hear that our War Office tested Sir William Sandling's gas at Aldershot yesterday, and a number of experts agreed that it failed to come up to expectations."

"Oh, is that so?" she murmured thought fully. Then she laughed.

"Of course—what else would they say?" she cried. "You see, Mr.—Mr. Odd-eyes, I under stand these things. Well, I hope you are right, and that the Bolsheviki have not secured that gas, because the day may not be far distant when you will be more than willing to supply it to Germany for your own protection as well as hers. I don't believe for an instant that England knows her real danger, or she would never allow the Moscow gang to undermine her authority here."

"Even a friendly critic like you, madam, must admit that Sir William's death has been avenged without much loss of time," put in Dunkeld, who was longing to bid her hold her pert tongue. Even the most amiable of men resents being kicked violently in the stomach.

"You cannot be certain that those two men are the actual criminals," she snapped.

"Certainty is rare in cases of murder, but they, at least, seemed to have no doubt. They went to their death rather than face the charge."

After that there was silence. No matter how flippant English-speaking Beatrice might be, German-born Bertha had cause for anxiety. These British policemen were stubborn fellows with fixed ideas. It was quite possible that if they disliked anyone, even a well-dressed and pretty young woman, they could make life most unpleasant for her.

During the next few hours, probably for the first time in her active existence, she found her self relegated to a position of complete unimportance.

Even when Sheldon questioned her as to various matters she was well aware that her statements were merely being checked up by a wider knowledge of the very persons and events whereof she spoke. She was not detained in custody. At a reasonable hour a room was provided for her in a quiet hotel. Next morning Sheldon took her to London. After a day's respite, though forbidden to go near the Welbeck Street house again, following a brief interview with a magistrate in Bow Street she was deported to Germany, quite unostentatiously, but with a stern warning that if ever she came back to England she would find herself in prison.

She had not even the gratification of knowing that Sheldon lost no time in ringing up Furneaux. There might, he thought, be some grain of fact in her taunt that the decoys who took ship from Leith were really carrying important information.

The little man bore the insult stoically.

"Please reassure the dear girl on that point," he said. "Those lads and their belongings were gone through with a fine comb, or its equivalent, in so far as documents were concerned. They are mere cyphers. All names and addresses among their papers have been recorded a dozen times already. Will you tell Dunkeld that Captain Mannering and young Hardacre will identify the dead birds to-morrow morning at nine? I suppose Miss Betty has not seen them since their regrettable accident?"

"No. I understand she was thoroughly knocked out, so a local doctor, chap named Lysaght, took her off to Foxton in his car."

"Good! I'm sure Dunkeld will keep her out of the inquest, which, in any case, should be adjourned for a fortnight. By that time the whole affair will be a wash-out in the public mind. Sorry I shan't see you in York. The Chief wants me to visit Glasgow. I suppose I am being punished now for some long-forgotten crime."

Furneaux arranged to share a late meal with the two younger men before they left Edinburgh that night. He was waiting for them in the foyer of the hotel about nine o'clock when he heard Tags barking loudly. The dog trotted in ahead of his friends. Evidently he was very pleased about something.

"Well," cried the detective, "what's in the wind now? Has he seen a haggis?"

"No," grinned Mannering; "he has just heard his mistress's voice."

"Do you mean to tell me you caused that unfortunate young woman to be dragged out of bed to listen to your maunderings over the phone?"

"Evidently you're one of the die-hards who regard the modern girl as not fitted to use a vote," was the calm retort. "You may not believe me, but Brother Frank will vouch for the fact that his sister said she had just eaten a large section of veal and ham pie, and is now drinking coffee and smoking a cigarette. The Lysaghts are Christians who live in Yorkshire."

"I know where they are compelled to live, but they cannot possibly be Christians, or they would never allow Miss Hardacre to gorge on veal and ham, coffee and nicotine at this ungodly hour. I must look up Lysaght. He struck me as being a decent scout, but I am beginning to suspect his diploma."

*   *   *   *   *

Early next morning young Hardacre telephoned to his employers and secured another day's leave. When he and Mannering had carried out a disagreeable task at the mortuary, they lost not a second in hiring a car, which took them swiftly to Foxton.

Betty herself ran forth to greet them. She kissed her brother and held out a hand to Mannering. She was rather pale, which, all things considered, both adventures and diet, was not surprising, yet she suddenly grew scarlet and covered her confusion by stooping to lift a vociferous dog.

Mannering, too, became a trifle self-conscious, the fact being, of course, that each had surprised a look in the other's eyes that spoke volumes. The incident was helpful, too. When, after luncheon, the two found themselves alone in the orchard which formed part of Lysaght's domain, Mannering took Betty by the shoulders.

"Dear!" he said, "are you glad to see me again?"

She met his gaze fearlessly.

"Yes, very glad and happy," she murmured.

"Dear!" he said again, as though the word were sweet on his lips, "will you marry me?"

She drew his face down and kissed him.

"That is my answer," she cooed.

After that, for a minute or so, their conversation was hardly intelligible. They were brought back to the everyday world by a distant voice.

"Captain Mannering!" it cried. "You're wanted on the telephone, he-he! Long distance, ha-ha!"

"Come along, Betty!" said the devout lover. "You may as well hear what the call is about, though wild horses won't drag me away from Foxton to-day."

It was Furneaux.

"I'm fed to the teeth with Glasgow and its Communists," he announced, "so I'm just taking a peep into the Elysian fields, a perfectly correct trope, because Mrs. Lysaght said you were in the garden with Betty. What about it?"

"Well, everything in the garden is lovely."

"Hugged her good and hard?"

"Yes."

"What a world! My hearty congratulations, young man! You haven't lost any time, but I doubt if you'd find a nicer girl if you searched all England."

"You're right, of course. You always are. I wish you'd put in a good word for me."

"Is Betty there?"

"Listening in!"

"Naturally! Very well! Tell her the Yard approves, and any bright young fellow has to go a long way before he gets a better testimonial than that. Well, well! Take care of her. She's worth it. If she has any complaints she must ring up 'Victoria 7000," and you'll hear of it, damned quick! Good-bye-ee!"

CHAPTER 15: WHEREIN REALITY SUPPLANTS ROMANCE

BETTY did not go back to her West Yorkshire College of Technology. Mannering made it quite clear that a courtship which had developed so rapidly should be rounded off by a speedy wedding. But Betty hung back a little, and ultimately made this ardent wooer see that it would be vastly more discreet if they evaded the public eye by permitting all inquests and judicial proceedings to be merged in "Yesterday's Seven Thousand Years" before getting married.

The affair at York was hushed up with singular success; the criminals were dead, and a public expose would have served no good purpose. The attempted kidnapping and subsequent gunplay at Foxton could, not be dealt with so simply. Once set in motion, the law of the land had to take its course. Betty figured as an important witness for the Crown at Leeds Autumn Assizes. For a couple of days she received all the publicity usually reserved for a cinema star.

Doolan was awarded ten years' penal servitude. The man who fired at Superintendent Dunkeld and the Foxton constable was let off with eighteen months' hard labour because his right hand had practically been blown to pieces by Dunkeld's 12-bore. The driver of the car, too, having suffered most unpleasant injuries, escaped with a light sentence, but Pierre Girard, callous scoundrel that he was, merely yelled" Vive Lenin et l'anarchie!" when given seven years.

Seeing that Betty was due a holiday at the expense of a Government which never has a sixpence to spare for any such purpose, she was brought to London for a while to help in sorting the scientific papers found in the

Welbeck Street house, and assist Sir William Sandling's trustees. Mannering, of course, took care that her principal occupation during those few weeks should be a close and sustained study of his own admirable qualities as her prospective partner for life.

After the Assizes, Betty ran her fiancé over to Foxton to attend a most interesting ceremony. The leading residents in that part of the North Riding were entertaining Superintendent Dunkeld at a public luncheon. The Lord Lieutenant, who presided, not only handed to the guest of honour what the newspapers described as "a handsome cheque," but announced that a visit to Buckingham Palace would follow in due course, because the superintendent would be "decorated" for his "fearless and unswerving devotion to duty."

Betty was puzzled by a special request that she should bring Tags to this feast, but she understood when at one stage of the proceedings a film showing the fight between Dunkeld and the motor bandits and her own rescue was staged. The Home Office would not allow the picture to be exhibited in public until the men in the car were convicted and sentenced, for the very sound reason that such a piece of evidence broadcasted before their trial might have had most undesirable legal consequences. It was, in fact, produced at Foxton for the first time.

Betty was roundly cheered by everybody present when, on the screen, she showed how she had passed through a great ordeal smiling and unruffled. Being a woman, she broke down and wept, but Mrs. Lysaght comforted her by giggling loudly: "My dear, there's nothing to cry about, he-he! Every young woman in England envies you, ha-ha! Did you ever find out—he-he!—who the funny little man on the motor-bicycle was, ha-ha?"

Tags barked, probably because the film had excited him, and several people laughed. Even the Lord

Lieutenant unbent when Dunkeld whispered an explanation.

Now, Mrs. Lysaght had actually met Furneaux in her own house. He had travelled specially from Town to attend this pleasant gathering, and was seated opposite the lady at that very moment. At first he thought she was amusing herself at his expense, but the secret had been well kept, so he rose to the occasion.

"No, ma'am," he said, in a penetrating whisper, "his identity has not been made known. Though he may have looked grotesque, he was really a hero. When someone told him that Captain Mannering had a prior claim, he did not remove his goggles. Miss Betty, therefore, can never know the chance she lost! Is not that the stuff of which true romance is made? He probably was, as you say, a 'funny little man '—but he is a bachelor, too, and now may remain one all his days—so my sympathetic heart aches for him!"

Dr. Lysaght fumed for a minute or so. Then he laughed. A tactful woman is not necessarily a good housewife, and his better half was deservedly famous for the way in which she ran their establishment.

At last there came a day in late autumn when Robert Mannering and Elisabeth Ann ("Betty") Hardacre were united in the bonds of holy matrimony, as the finely worded phrase of the Church has it. The West Riding village where Betty's people lived was so remote that they contrived to elude both newspaper reporters and photographers, because Mannering had pro cured a special licence. But they could not dodge Scotland Yard, there being a clear understanding that they were to be entertained at Pucci's while passing through London after the ceremony.

A somewhat noteworthy and quite unusual company assembled in the little Soho restaurant. The Chief, who presided, brought Mrs. Winter. Colonel Westoby and Superintendent Dunkeld were there with their respective wives, while a Cabinet Minister was present incognito. It was probably for his benefit that Furneaux, taking advantage of a lull before Winter proposed the health of the newly married couple, said confidentially: "While you are about it, Chief, you might tell this distinguished gathering what really happened before we put 'paid' to the final account of Messieurs Luvitsky and Vereschagin."

Winter seemed to weigh the point seriously. After a slight pause, which Furneaux described later as a cheap stage effect, he evidently deter mined to postpone the toast of the evening, and, without rising, accepted his colleague's challenge.

"It's by way of being a departmental secret," he said, "but it is known already to a good many people, so a slight widening of the circle cannot do much harm. The truth is that we were by no means out of danger when those two men were wiped out at York. They had secured the formula, and retained possession even in death!"

He glanced around the table to see how many of his hearers appreciated the gravity of this statement. Betty and her husband and the Cabinet Minister reacted to the test instantly. They were genuinely surprised, and would certainly have been startled if the Chief had not chosen that moment to help himself to a second glass of port, thus showing that he, at any rate, was not greatly perturbed. Dunkeld and the other men from the Yard knew the facts already. As for the three middle-aged women who had just heard something which might have sent a shudder of horror through the whole civilised world, they were not even interested. A formula! What was a formula? A sort of prescription which only a chemist could read, and resulted in some noxious mixture in a bottle, to be taken with water three times daily.

"Some of us feared that something of the sort might have happened," went on Winter. "Mr. Dunkeld was the first to draw attention to the almost maniacal disorder in which Luvitsky and his companion left Sir William Sandling's personal belongings in the farmhouse. Viewed in connection with their well-laid plans and successful flight, it struck him as a method of concealment rather than an indication of hurried search. Then Mr. Furneaux was convinced that the pair of scoundrels who took ship at Leith were rather too conscious of their own safety. Finally, Miss Bertha von Buren blurted out to Sheldon some well-founded suspicions of the truth. So, as nothing of any vital importance was found in the suitcases recovered from the train at York, and it was quite impracticable to search then and there a couple of large vans packed with heavy luggage from floors to roofs, both Dunkeld and Sheldon impressed on me the importance of thorough measures being taken to safeguard the Russians' baggage at King's Cross."

"Of course," he interpolated, after a slight pause, "Mr. Furneaux had telephoned me to the same effect some hours earlier from Edinburgh. Indeed, much as I dislike and disapprove of sheer guesswork in departmental inquiries, I am bound to admit that my small friend might almost have arranged the details with Luvitsky himself, so closely did the facts accord with his imaginative reasoning."

"What a charming tribute!" sighed Furneaux.

The Cabinet Minister obviously felt that the Chief had expressed himself awkwardly.

"I think I am beginning to see light," he said. "Let me say now, Mr. Furneaux, that, on Mr. Winter's strong recommendation, the Home Secretary is about to put forward your name for the C.V.O., and Mrs. Mannering's for the C.B.E."

"That most satisfactory statement clears the ground, at any rate," purred Winter. "It is plain to every eye, too, that I must make way for the chorus of congratulations which will break out almost instantly. So I bring you at a bound, so to speak, to King's Cross late at night, when every available man from the Yard closed in on the twenty or more known Bolshies who awaited the arrival of that train. They were hustled out of the way so promptly and quietly that very few of the general public knew anything about it, and not a line appeared in the newspapers. There was only one leather trunk of importance, and we found it quite easily, because, although the lock had been forced and replaced by a small padlock, the key picked up on the moor by P.C. Paxton – "

He hesitated, and looked at Dunkeld.

"Sergeant Paxton," came the correction.

"Exactly. Well, that key fitted the broken lock. In the bag, among some valuable memoranda and records of monetary payments, we discovered a chemical analysis in the handwriting of Sir William Sandling. I am told it corresponds word for word, symbol for symbol, with the entry in the locked diary which Mrs. Mannering will remember for many a day. The quite allowable deduction is that Sir William carried this working copy for the purposes of the open-air experiments made in a rabbit-warren on the morning of his death, that Luvitsky and Vereschagin saw him consulting it, and that he was killed because he refused to give it up."

He turned forthwith to the Cabinet Minister.

"And now, sir," he said, "I have much pleasure in asking you to propose—"

"Oh no, you haven't!" vowed the great man emphatically. "Just for a moment I forgot the international reputation you and Mr. Furneaux have as experts in the gentle art of leg-pulling. Of course, I wanted to supplement what you had to say by the pleasant announcement that His Majesty's Government does occasionally pay honour where honour is due. . . . My friends, if I may usurp Mr. Winter's position for even one second, I call on him to toast the bride and bridegroom!"

*　　*　　*　　*　　*

Not even in the austere atmosphere of an assize court in the North-Eastern Circuit are things always what they seem. Captain and Mrs. Mannering, prowling about

Marseilles one day in December during their wedding tour in the South of France, chose an attractive-looking café on the Cannebière for luncheon. They were waited on by Pierre Girard! He had been released as soon as the affair began to be forgotten.

Recognition was immediate and mutual.

"*Oui, m'sieu' et 'dame*," said he affably. "*C'est drôle, n'est-ce p'as? Mais, vraiment, c'est la vie*! I am vat you call 'good boy' nowa days, an' my wife she ver' glad. . . . Ze plat du jour is bouiia-baisse, mek' of ze feesh. Some Eengleesh like, some not. Try a leetle!"

THE END

Resurrected Press Mysteries From Louis Tracy

The Albert Gate Mystery

Four men murdered and a fortune in diamonds belonging to the Turkish Sultan stolen, while the Foreign Office official in charge has gone missing. Was it a common jewelry theft or was it a case of international intrigue? This is the question that barrister detective Reginald Brett must solve.

The Bartlett Mystery

When Ronald Tower is murdered on his way to a bridge game on the yacht Sans Souci it at first appears a common crime. But as Rex Carshaw finds, a tragic case of mistaken identity leads to political scandal among the rich and powerful of New York.

The Strange Case of Mortimer Fenley

When the wealthy Mortimer Fenley is struck down by a shot from an express rifle on the steps of his mansion, detectives Winter and Furneaux of Scotland Yard must find the culprit. Was it the artist who claimed he was painting a picture at the time of the shot? The disaffected younger son? Or is there another suspect?

The Stowmarket Mystery

For five generations the Fergus-Hume family has been cursed. Each of the baronets has met a violent end. When the fifth baronet is found slain by a ceremonial Japanese dagger, suspicion falls on his cousin David. It falls to barrister detective Reginald Brett to prove his innocence and find the real murder in a case that spans two continents and as many centuries.

Visit www.resurrectedpress.com

Resurrected Press Mysteries by J. S. Fletcher

The Orange-Yellow Diamond

When an elderly pawnbroker is murdered in the London parish of Paddington, a young, down on his luck writer is accused of the crime. But then it's found the pawnbroker had had in his possession an extraordinary South African diamond worth over eighty-thousand pounds — a diamond that's now missing. It falls to Melky Rubenstein to unravel the mystery and prove the young man's innocence.

The Middle Temple Murder

When an elderly man's body is found on the steps of chambers in the Midde Temple, one of the Inns of Court, it falls to newspaperman Frank Spargo and Detective-Sergeant Rathbury to solve the crime. The murdered man, for indeed it was murder, was found with no money or identification on his person except for a piece of paper with the name and address of a young barrister. Who is the victim? Why was he killed? Who is the murderer?

Scarhaven Keep

Bassett Oliver, the famed actor, has gone missing. When Oliver fails to show for a rehearsal, aspiring playwright Richard Copplestone finds himself sent to the small village of Scarhaven on the northern coast of England to track down the actors movements. What he finds is mystery. Find the answers as Copplestone unravels the mystery of Scarhaven Keep.

Visit www.resurrectedpress.com

Resurrected Press Mysteries by Fergus Hume

The Green Mummy

Professor Braddock hoped to compare the burial practices of the Egyptians with those of the ancient Peruvians with his latest acquisition, the mummy of the last Inca, Caxas. But on arrival, the packing case proved to hold not the mummy, but the body of his assistant Sidney Bolton. It falls to Archie Hope to discover the murderer if he is to marry the professors step-daughter, Lucy Kendal. Who killed Bolton and where is the mummy? Was it the sea captain Hervey? The mysterious Don Pedro? Cockatoo the Polynesian servant? The professor, himself? And what has become of the emeralds? These are the questions that Hope must answer amongst the secrets of the past in The Green Mummy.

The Mystery of a Hansom Cab

"Truth is said to be stranger than fiction, and certainly the extraordinary murder which took place in Melbourne Friday morning goes a long way towards verifying that saying." Thus opens The Mystery of a Hansom Cab, the best selling mystery of the nineteenth century. When a man is found dead in a hansom cab one of Melbourne's leading citizens is accused of the murder. He pleads his innocence, yet refuses to give an alibi. It falls to a determined lawyer and an intrepid detective to find the truth, revealing long kept secrets along the way. Fergus Hume's first and perhaps most famous mystery... The Mystery Of A Hansom Cab.

Visit www.resurrectedpress.com

Resurrected Press Mysteries from the Dr. John Thorndyke Series

Dr. John Thorndyke - Lecturer on Medical Jurisprudence and Forensic Medicine. Before Bones, before CSI, before Quincy, M.E– there was Dr. John Thorndyke solving the most baffling cases of Edwardian London using the latest tools of medical science. Read about his cases in:

The Eye of Osiris
John Bellingham, noted Egyptologist has vanished not once but twice in the same day. Now Dr, Thorndyke must unravel the tangled claims on his estate, solve the riddle of the missing man and find the "Eye of Osiris".

The Mystery of 31 New Inn
When Dr. Jervis is whisked away in a coach with no windows to an unknown location to treat a man in a coma from undivulged causes it is Dr. Thorndyke who must come up with the solution.

The Red Thumb Mark
The first of Dr. Thorndyke's cases finds him trying to prove the innocence of a young man accused of being a diamond thief despite the fact that his finger print was found at the scene of the crime.

John Thorndyke's Cases
More cases of medical mysteries as told by his trusted assistant Jervis, M.D. Eight stories of crime and deduction in Edwardian London.

Visit www.resurrectedpress.com

Resurrected Press Mysteries by John R. Watson & Arthur J. Rees

The Hampstead Mystery

High Court Justice Sir Horace Fewbanks found shot dead in his Hampstead home, a butler with a criminal past, a scorned lover and a hint of scandal. These are the elements of the Hampstead Mystery that Detective Inspector Chippenfield of Scotland Yard must unravel with the assistance of the ambitious Detective Rolfe. But will he be able to sort out the tangled threads of this case and arrest the culprit before he is upstaged by the celebrated gentleman detective Crewe. Follow the details of this amazing case at it plays out across Hampstead, London and Scotland until it reaches a stunning conclusion in the courts of the Old Bailey.

The Mystery of the Downs

When Harry Marsland was caught in a sudden down pour he sought shelter at Cliff Farm. Met at the door by a young woman clearly expecting someone else he is only too glad to get inside to wait out the storm. When they hear a noise upstairs in the deserted house they investigate only to discover the body of the farm's owner, Frank Lumsden, dead of a gunshot wound. Who then, killed Lumsden, and why? Who was the woman expecting and did she have any roll in the murder? These are the questions that private detective Crewe must answer in The Mystery of the Downs.

Visit www.resurrectedpress.com

Other Resurrected Press Mysteries

Mysteries on a Train

Before the Orient Express there was:

The Rome Express by Arthur Griffiths
A man is found dead in his first class sleeping compartment on the express from Rome to Paris. Who was his murderer? The Countess? The English General? His brother the clergy man? The maid who has disappeared? Is the French justice system up to solving the crime? Read about it in The Rome Express.

The Passenger from Calais by Arthur Griffiths
Colonel Basil Annesley finds he is the only passenger on the train from Calais to Lucerne. That is until a mysterious woman shows up at the last minute to book a compartment. Who is after her? What is her secret? Is she a criminal or a victim? Read about it in The Passenger from Calais

Visit us at www.resurrectedpress.com

About Resurrected Press

A division of Intrepid Ink, LLC, Resurrected Press is dedicated to bringing high quality, vintage books back into publication. See our entire catalogue and find out more at www.ResurrectedPress.com.

About Intrepid Ink, LLC

Intrepid Ink, LLC provides full publishing services to authors of fiction and non-fiction books, eBooks and websites. From editing to formatting, from publishing to marketing, Intrepid Ink gets your creative works into the hands of the people who want to read them. Find out more at www.IntrepidInk.com.